On the Citizen House:

A Disquisitive Fiction

By David Grant

www.CommonLotProductions.net

Paperback edition
ISBN 978-0-9992084-1-0

It is accepted as democratic
when public offices are allocated by lot;
and as oligarchic
when they are filled by election.
Aristotle {Politics. 4.1294b}

A picnic, early autumn, at a state park in the chaparral foothills of California's central coast. Signs posted: 'Fire danger: Extreme!'

Anthony, nine, African-American, plays catch. Despite his large top-of-the-line baseball mitt, he misses often. The other children make allowances, sending soft, easy-to-catch pitches his way. He whines, makes excuses. He holds onto the ball longer than he needs to.

One by one, the mothers take their children home. Anthony and his mother are last to leave. Absent mindedly, she tosses her cigarette. The duff quickly catches fire. She tries smothering it, too late, quickly becoming a blaze. She grabs her son, jumps in the car and guns it out of the tinderbox forest.

On the way home she instructs her son.

ANTHONY'S MOTHER: If anyone asks you, say that you were playing with matches. If you don't do that, I will be taken away. I won't see you for years.

The police arrive to the house, an extravagance, cantilevered over a canyon. They deliver Anthony's baseball mitt, scorched. They interrogate his mother.

Chiding Anthony, his mother shakes the mitt at her son. Anthony's father mumbles an apology, shrinking.

ANTHONY'S FATHER: The poor boy. He has a disability.

Anthony snatches the mitt from his mother and shouts at the police.

ANTHONY: You got it dirty! You got it dirty!

The fire escapes the forest. Houses ignite. People die.

That evening his parents host highbrow friends whom they have invited to watch a movie on their big screen: Robert Bresson's classic, 'Au Hasard, Balthasar'. The life story of a donkey.

They laugh at the cruelty in it. The sexual misbehavior of the animal's owners. The hooligans who pour oil on a curve in the road, laughing to see motorcyclists tumble.

The senseless beatings of the innocent donkey.

They analyze the film dispassionately.

1

SMILING HIGHBROW: The title amuses. I wonder why it isn't translated? 'Balthazar, At Random?'

STOCKY HIGHBROW: The irony is stronger in French.

SKINNY HIGHBROW: His life is no more random than ours.

STOCKY HIGHBROW: Not to say ours isn't.

SMILING HIGHBROW: We owe our station in life to birth. To randomness.

STOCKY HIGHBROW: 'Hasard' the French, random or chance. 'Hazard', the English, danger. What life brings us, both ways, just a little different tack.

SKINNY HIGHBROW: All of us are ordinary. Where are the exceptions?

SMILING HIGHBROW: Ah, a heretic!

STOCKY HIGHBROW: The fittest rule.

SKINNY HIGHBROW: We all have to breathe.

STOCKY HIGHBROW: Bring on the existential!

SMILING HIGHBROW: Back to the movie! You're ruining the seduction scene where the old rich man gets the young starving girl.

SKINNY HIGHBROW: Ordinary, as I said. What we are.

Unnoticed, Little Anthony creeps unsteadily around the room. Stationing himself behind a whispering couple he eavesdrops upon their prattle.

WHISPERING WOMAN: Poor little Anthony.

WHISPERING MAN: A Balthazar himself.

WHISPERING WOMAN: Hobbled.

WHISPERING MAN: The disease.

WHISPERING WOMAN: Tragic.

WHISPERING MAN: The way his parents cover it. 'Only clumsy. Growing pains.'

WHISPERING WOMAN: Degenerative.

WHISPERING MAN: How fast?

WHISPERING WOMAN: In a few years, a wheelchair. Then no one knows.

Anthony jumps out from behind, surprising them. They are embarrassed. Anthony sneers.

2

In the chaparral the fire rages on.

*FOUR DECADES LATER. THE NOT-TOO-DISTANT FUTURE.
JUNE.*

*In the Blue Ridge Mountains of western North Carolina
Josephine, 28, Euro-American, sits in a classroom full of people
taking the civics test to qualify for the lottery pool for the Citizen
House.*

*She labors to answer the multiple choice test, but the letters
squiggle.*

*Time is running out. She's tired. To her, the last question
looks like: 'Nawe tmo rights in Declaratiou of Imbeqembemce.' The
choices as: 'lite,' 'liderty' and 'qursuit of qroqerty.' At a loss, she
randomly circles 'lite' and 'liderty.'*

After the test, she gets a ride home with a Neighbor.
NEIGHBOR: Audacious child! What gave you the idea?
You got no chance, taking that test.
JOSEPHINE: They say we all got a chance. Every one of us.
Everybody's in it, That's what they say.
NEIGHBOR: Blue sky dreamers, that's all they are. If you
won that lottery, you'd just make a fool of yourself up there in
Washington.
JOSEPHINE: Guess you better just not read the newspapers.
NEIGHBOR: You're right there. Nothing but lies, them
papers.
JOSEPHINE: Good for nothing, hey?
NEIGHBOR: Durn tootin'.
JOSEPHINE: You're sure?
Neighbor reconsiders
NEIGHBOR: Well … something to wipe with.

SEPTEMBER

*Josephine clocks out of her waitressing job and drags herself
back to her trailer park home. When she opens the front door, a
stink assaults her. She takes four steps and opens the bathroom*

door. The commode has overflowed, clogged with newspaper. She looks in the cabinet under the sink. Empty.

Her son appears.

JOSEPHINE'S SON: Sorry, mom, I…

She hugs him.

JOSEPHINE: Sorry myself, honey. I should have bought an extra roll.

Her son blushes at the mess.

SON: Possum got a hen. But I plugged that possum.

Smiling at him, she leads him to the kitchen.

JOSEPHINE: Let me take a look at the mail before we deal with all that.

She opens the mail. Turns jubilant.

JOSEPHINE: We may be down, but we're not out. Not by a long shot. We may be ordinary but we can do extra-ordinary things. Like turn that possum into a stew.

She hugs her son harder.

On the northern coast of California, a wood fire blazes under a hot tub.

Anthony, 49, rolls in his wheelchair up to the tub and lifts himself into the stew with a half-dozen of his naked multi-hued friends.

ANTHONY: Couldn't wait for me, could you? Just had to jump in first.

SALLOW FRIEND: We didn't mean anything by it.

ANTHONY: Of course not.

Anthony hums.

ANTHONY: 'I hear the gentle voices calling, Old Black Joe'.

He fakes a shuffle, drops his voice an octave.

ANTHONY: Ole darkie crip just natchally be de las'.

ROSY FRIEND: Not funny.

ANTHONY: Ha. Just saying… we're all cooked.

ROSY FRIEND: How are you going to stand it, Anthony? Having to hobnob with the hoi poloi?

ANTHONY: True, it won't be easy. It's helter skelter. Nothing but freshmen. Like frogs in a slowly heating cauldron.

4

ROSY FRIEND: Surrounded by cannibals.

ANTHONY: The corporate piranha. Calling themselves progressive.

SALLOW FRIEND: Scum. Even yelling 'Power To The People'.

ANTHONY: Right, power for all the causes -- justice, prosperity, responsibility, tolerance...

SALLOW FRIEND: Cooperation, peace...

ANTHONY: But they overlook the core political value of modern civilization. Liberty. Only liberty gives substance and form to all the other values.

SALLOW FRIEND: And thus we call ourselves libertarians.

BRONZE FRIEND: The irony, to be criticized for freedom.

ROSY FRIEND: History's full of it. The Citizen House is just another dollop.

BRONZE FRIEND: Or trollop.

ANTHONY: It'll be sleeping with strange bedfellows for all of us.

They chuckle salaciously.

Wearing high heels and a frumpy dress, Josephine enters the household of the family that has agreed to host her. Just outside Washington. Bethesda, Maryland.

HOST WIFE: Can we call you 'Jo'? I've got a great aunt Josephine. We always called her 'Jo'.

JOSEPHINE: I, unh... I've always answered to Josephine.

HOST WIFE: Not going to be 'a regular Jo'?

JOSEPHINE: I'll be spending weekends back home. My mother's taking care of my son.

HOST WIFE: Well, OK. Let me show you the house.

They traipse through rooms of mementos, the booty and plunder from The Hosts' years as international aid workers.

Entering one of the bathrooms, Josephine stumbles.

JOSEPHINE: It's these high heels. Do you mind if I take them off?

HOST WIFE: I gave up foot-binders long ago.

They enter a bedroom. On the wall is a big hand-lettered sign in Hebrew script: 'Baruch haba!'

HOST WIFE: 'Welcome!' It's so exciting, Jo, to have you. We've never known anyone from North Carolina. We've kind of neglected our own country. Been to forty others. I-N-G-Os. Humanitarian assistance.

JOSEPHINE: Six bathrooms, did you say?

HOST WIFE: Our traveling days are over. At least for now. The kids need stability. So... we write grants.

Josephine only smiles.

HOST WIFE: The quiet type? You'll have to learn to talk. A legislator! Isn't it a wonder?

The Daughter rushes in.

HOST DAUGHTER: Is she the hillbilly, mom?

HOST WIFE: Daughter! Who taught you that word?

HOST DAUGHTER: At school. They said she was on TV. A hillbilly, they said.

Host Wife and Host Husband lie in bed.

HOST WIFE: Whatever were we thinking? Was there a mix-up in assignments?

HOST HUSBAND: She's good with the kids.

HOST WIFE: They say only one-third of the populace can name the three branches of government.

HOST HUSBAND: She passed the civics test. No more difficult than the one for a driver's license. And they'll benefit from weeks of orientation.

HOST WIFE: She's a perfect example of the famous 'ordinary citizen'. Never would have had a voice before.

HOST HUSBAND: There are, though, a few, still... of the type A. The type that could have competed and could have won... election. She'll have to face them.

HOST WIFE: We'll tutor her. Introduce her to UBI.

HOST HUSBAND: Right.

He drowses.

HOST HUSBAND: Or Mini-Max.

HOST WIFE: We'll be her mentors.

HOST HUSBAND: We'll teach.

HOST WIFE: She'll learn.

HOST HUSBAND: She'll...

6

HOST WIFE: They'll...
Sleep.

JUNE

Inside the chamber of the Citizen House, a few representatives make the effort to engage with Anthony as he berates and cajoles. In the deep back benches Josephine sits alone, alert and listening.

ANTHONY: Why shouldn't we unshackle science? It was the science of statistics — the Law of Large Numbers — that undergirded the argument to use sortition. Now that 'everybody's in', so to speak, why shouldn't that scientific method of inquiry be allowed to make us all better human beings? Through eugenic improvement!

TALL REP: I ask the obvious. At the Nuremberg Trials, the Nazi's legal defense entered as evidence the book 'Passing of the Great Race'. The American author promotes euthanasia for the purpose of racial cleansing. The Nazis justified their actions by pointing out that there was nothing unique at that time about it.

ANTHONY: It is true. In the 1920's leaders of the top black colleges supported eugenics. They said that only 'The Talented Tenth' -- of all races -- should breed. W. E. B. Du Bois said '... only fit blacks should procreate.'

SHORT REP: The U.S. had led the way.

TALL REP: We will not make that mistake again. It's the other end of abortion.

Tall Rep shakes a sheaf of paper. She is indignity personified.

TALL REP: I have here an entry from the blog of a group calling itself 'Lobak'. It's an acronym for 'Loosely Organized Bunch Against Kollectivism'. That's with a 'K'.

A smirk.

TALL REP: Cleverly self-deprecating. Urbane. Erudite.

A hint of jeer.

TALL REP: Sophomoric. Get this.

Reading.

TALL REP: 'Plato suggested a positive form of eugenics. He thought a guardian class could be bred through selective mating. The U.S. was practicing eugenics a decade before the Nazis misused it. Practice in the U.S. inspired them.'

SHORT REP: This Lobak must be ashamed of what they are doing. None of them use their names. They identify themselves only by 'Lobak' followed by a number.

Tall Rep shrugs assent.

SHORT REP: So is theirs a progressive or a regressive position?

TALL REP: They consider themselves libertarians. But few of us care about the labels. Only a few of us are constrained by party affiliation. Most here are independents.

SHORT REP: The People are not going to rally behind ideological extremes.

ANTHONY: Maybe so. But don't kid yourselves… Predictability happens.

Newspaper headlines, talking heads, Twitter feeds, social media. All a'buzz.

BUZZ: Eugenics is unconstitutional.

BUZZ: At odds with The People's wellbeing.

BUZZ: Is progress.

BUZZ: Is not.

BUZZ: Is hell.

BUZZ: Heaven.

BUZZ: Is not.

BUZZ: Is.

BUZZ: Is not.

BUZZ: Is.

Et cetera.

Late evening, Josephine peruses the book shelves at the Bethesda home. Standing in a place of honor is a copy of Thomas Paine's Agrarian Justice. The Wife enters and lovingly handles the book for Josephine to see.

HOST WIFE: Paine argued for capital grants provided at the age of majority. He paired it with asset-based egalitarianism.

8

Josephine nods, sleepily.
HOST WIFE: This edition, 1796, is valued at $600.
JOSEPHINE: Yeah, yeah... Teaching me again. Look, I think I know...

From his sumptuous apartment in upper northwest Washington, Anthony video-chats with his hot tub friends in California.
SALLOW FRIEND: We are only talking about making a law, after all, not amending the Constitution. We already lost the first round in that regard.
ROSY FRIEND: I still don't see how the Court convinced itself that 'elect' meant 'by random selection'.
SALLOW FRIEND: Blame the Brits. In the Oxford English Dictionary 'ballot' has two entries. To vote by some secret method. And... To select by lot.
ROSY FRIEND: Ballot, hey? What about 'bullet'?
ANTHONY: Now, now. Beware the Chekovian edict. We're still in the first year, the first act, of this Citizen House. Mention of a weapon here requires blood flow later on.
BRONZE FRIEND: How about fake blood? Would that count?
ROSY FRIEND: We could splatter it around after we use one of those replica guns?
BRONZE FRIEND: Like those that caused the police to accidentally kill a few?
SALLOW FRIEND: Thinking they were... Unh, what is the term? Active shooters?
ROSY FRIEND: Terrorists.
ANTHONY: Maybe. Maybe so. But we'll just have to see how our dramatic structure turns out. Eventually. In the end.
BRONZE FRIEND: Anthony, if the so-called 'statistically-representative' group in the Citizen House won't pass a bill that lifts restrictions on legitimate eugenics-oriented research, then you've got to advocate directly to The People.
ANTHONY: Eugenics is already consumer driven. We just need to counter the negative history. Unlike the Nazis, modern

eugenics is market based. Children are increasingly regarded as made-to-order.

ROSY FRIEND: All you need is one percent of the voting populace. To be actively committed to eugenics. Or even less. A million, say. Less than one-third of one percent. Then with those shock troops you can persuade many others to give passive support. You could even get a petition going. If you use the right someone to hand out a petition, people will sign anything

SALLOW FRIEND: Might be a pretty face. Or someone in horned rim glasses. Or a hunk of cheesecake

ROSY FRIEND: Cheesecake?

ANTHONY: Beefcake.

SALLOW FRIEND: Unh, yeah. Or a fat person to a fat person.

ANTHONY: Obese to obese.

BRONZE FRIEND: You've got to have the facts right, too. But you do. Right?

Anthony winces, disdainful.

SALLOW FRIEND: Those three elements: an active core; a passive majority; and the facts. You've got a successful movement.

ROSY FRIEND: It's the end of June. Summer recess is about to start. You can barnstorm. No reason not to. No fear of electoral consequences. None.

BRONZE FRIEND: At least one benefit of sortition. No constituents.

ROSY FRIEND: Just the right time to launch a 'Grassroots Campaign for Improvement of the Human Race'.

SALLOW FRIEND: You'll get a lot of attention, Anthony. Wheelchair bound. Of-color. Rhetorically-adroit as they say…

BRONZE FRIEND: It is likely that genetic engineering will soon be able to stop your deterioration. You may not be condemned to becoming a quadriplegic using a voice box.

SALLOW FRIEND: Stephen Hawking…

ROSY FRIEND: When they realize that your own personal future depends on genetic engineering, people will fall all over themselves.

SALLOW FRIEND: Right. And even more. Not only will it be able to prevent your further decline, but it also has the possibility to interrupt transmittal to your progeny.

ANTHONY: If I have any.

SALLOW FRIEND: By developing heritable germ-line therapy.

ROSY FRIEND: Take that to the bank. Slam dunk!

Anthony sloughs off his friends' arguments.

ANTHONY: But let's not be naïve. My skin color… We must base it on more than my personal condition.

They cogitate.

BRONZE FRIEND: How about someone to accompany you?

ROSY FRIEND: Someone to expand your base.

In his mind's eye Anthony peruses the Citizen House. He spies a back bench wallflower. She is wide-eyed, attentive.

ANTHONY: I've got someone in mind.

SALLOW FRIEND: Is she a Person-of-No-Color? Will she bring out the uneducated? The prejudiced?

ANTHONY: Yeah, sure. We need to balance our little juggernaut. You call her a Person-Of-No-Color? That's rich. Yes.

ROSY FRIEND: It's still a white-makes-right society. Call her your GEC.

BRONZE FRIEND: What's a GEC?

ROSY FRIEND: Balancing act. Gender-Ethnic-Class. G-E-C. Gecko.

SALLOW FRIEND: Croak, croak.

ANTHONY: What?

SALLOW FRIEND: Sound that a gecko makes.

ANTHONY: Is that so?

Anthony looks up from his wheelchair.

SALLOW FRIEND: We can use her.

Anthony snorts.

In the Host's living room, Josephine is again scanning the bookcase.

The Host Daughter comes in and sits near.

11

HOST DAUGHTER: Our school assignment is to determine the origin of explosives.

The daughter pulls a little flag from her bag. It is like an American flag except that the stripes normally red are black. And a skull-and-bones replaces the field of stars.

HOST DAUGHTER: Mom gave it to me. Mark Twain designed it as a protest against the United States colonizing the Philippines. That's why I chose this assignment.

JOSEPHINE: Did Mark Twain get the Nobel Prize?

The Host daughter pulls out her smartphone, taps. Nope.

JOSEPHINE: Wasn't Nobel the inventor of dynamite?

The Host daughter expands her arms grandly.

HOST DAUGHTER: One of history's great ironies! There are many. That's what our teacher said.

JOSEPHINE: So what else did you learn?

HOST DAUGHTER: Over a thousand years ago, Chinese Taoists, that's a kind of religion… They were looking for a way to live forever.

JOSEPHINE: Really?

HOST DAUGHTER: Yeah, they mixed up stuff, like druggists do today. They came up with a powder that fizzed. They called it fire medicine.

JOSEPHINE: Is that so?

HOST DAUGHTER: We learned the Chinese. Huoyao. I guess it didn't work to extend anyone's life. So then they used it for fireworks. Another kind of Big Bang.

The girl laughs. Josephine sits back, nonplussed.

HOST DAUGHTER: That's a joke. Teacher said so.

Host Wife walks in.

HOST WIFE: And what do we have here?

HOST DAUGHTER: Oh, just doing my assignment.

HOST WIFE: Weapons. TNT. Conventional. So much money.

Host wife is not amused.

HOST WIFE: The mean net wealth… All assets, all stuff owned by everybody…

HOST Daughter turns to Josephine.

HOST DAUGHTER: It's her thing.

HOST WIFE: It comes to around a quarter million dollars. Per person. To say nothing of the intellectual capital expended.

HOST DAUGHTER: I told you, Jo.

HOST WIFE: And they are prepared to blow it all up!

In the basement of the Citizen House at the cafeteria window from which hotdogs are served, Josephine bumps into Anthony.

ANTHONY: I believe you were interested in my presentation a few days ago?

JOSEPHINE: I'm learning a lot up here. About a lot of things.

ANTHONY: Really? Say so.

JOSEPHINE: Well, besides the debates, my hosts. In Bethesda. They call themselves 'my mentors.' Frankly though I'm beginning to feel claustrophobic. Sure, I'm thankful. But... it's about enough.

Anthony cackles.

ANTHONY: And now look at you. With a pork fat chili dog. Betraying your keepers.

JOSEPHINE: That's not funny. They're well-meaning. And besides, they don't keep kosher.

ANTHONY: Seculars, hey? Cadillac liberals. Hypocrites of the worst degree.

JOSEPHINE: You got something against their religion?

Anthony gives her the once-over, smarmy.

ANTHONY: Eat... your... hot… dog.

Josephine sits in her office at the Citizen House. Her smartphone dings.

From Anthony.

TEXT MESSAGE: Invitation to escape. Game, dame?

She cringes.

The door swings open.

Anthony rolls right in, big smile.

ANTHONY: It's my nationwide barnstorm, missy! To stir up support for libertarian eugenics. How about it?

Josephine withholds a gasp.

ANTHONY: If you've learned anything up here, you've learned that five hundred people cannot have a conversation. Time to hit the road! Meet The People! See some sights!

JOSEPHINE: What is this? Sweeping me off my feet? Not.

ANTHONY: We don't need court rulings. What we need is pressure from The People.

JOSEPHINE: And I'm supposed to help you...? Puh-leez.

She flicks her wrist in dismissal.

He rolls, snickering, out the door.

That night at dinner, Host Wife admonishes Josephine.

HOST WIFE: Jo, it's a trap. Eugenics! My God!

JOSEPHINE: Opportunity for fresh air, perhaps. See the country.

HOST WIFE: They want to use you. You must stay focused on progressive views. The only reason Anthony wants you, Jo, is because you are female and white. You're going to be his token!

JOSEPHINE: I'm not unaware.

HOST WIFE: Besides, Jo, this eugenics stuff is what the Nazis promoted. How the hell this African-American wheelchair-bound man could ever promote it is beyond me.

JOSEPHINE: Indeed.

HOST WIFE: But then he's one of the Ones-Who-Have-Made-It. Not the Homeys but the Owe-Me's. The O-W-H-M-I's.

Josephine smiles, appreciating Host Wife's little joke.

HOST WIFE: He played the market, sold short. Thanks to one of the ... 'little birdies' ... who tipped him off. He doesn't seem to mind having scored off the backs of loan sharks. But back to you. Jo, your dyslexia is genetically linked. You're asking for your own kind to be wiped out. My family happens to know a little something about 'genetic improvement', y'know?

That night in her bedroom, Josephine taps on her phone, struggling with auto correction, finally managing: R u relyl an OhMe?

She taps 'Send'.

To Anthony.

Next morning in the breakfast nook, Host Husband harps at Josephine.

HOST HUSBAND: So what about your own values, Jo? Income equality. And the Universal Basic Income, UBI? Or the MINI-MAXI? What about the limits, Jo?

Josephine puts up her hands. An OK, OK.

Host Husband hammers on.

HOST HUSBAND: You told us about your forebears, strong on FDR. He proposed an upper limit on income. Roosevelt didn't get his wish but maybe you can.

HOST WIFE: And there's the environment. Capping wages will diminish conspicuous consumption. That finances UBI. 'All men created equal' should mean a safety net for all.

HOST HUSBAND: Income inequality is the most dangerous social challenge facing us. Housing and education are the kernels of the white-black divide and the stubbornness of unforced segregation. Why shouldn't economics be the parameter? Rather than race or gender. To determine entitlements?

Josephine slams her hand on the table.

JOSEPHINE: You are the most exasperating well-meaning folk I've ever met. You could have stopped several paragraphs ago. I've had it with your mentoring. Yes, I'm telling Anthony that I'm going on his trip. But with my own agenda. To advocate for UBI.

Host Wife and Host Husband fall back on their heels.

JOSEPHINE: This cuts to the bone for me and my people. If Anthony can't handle it, tough. I'm laying it out as a deal breaker.

In a Washington sports club, Anthony hoists himself from his wheelchair into the hot tub.

ANTHONY: You've read my email. What do you think?

SALLOW FRIEND: Sounds like maybe we should invite this Josephine to join us?

BRONZE FRIEND: She has shown herself to be a little less malleable than you expected. Is that not so?

ROSY FRIEND: Just need to soften her up a bit. Time to turn cannibal?

Anthony shrugs, nonchalant.

ANTHONY: Her little show of independence indicates spunk. That can draw crowds. Useful.

Rosy Friend wrinkles his brow.

ROSY FRIEND: Possibly. But... more trouble than it's worth?

They let that sink in for a moment.

ANTHONY: Her nutty interventionist idea – income equality... That can provide cover. A populist diversion.

SALLOW FRIEND: A little spice.

Anthony dangles an imaginary puppet.

ANTHONY: Right.

Holed up in her bedroom, Josephine plows through the dictionary. Her fingers creep over words like 'fiscal', 'fiduciary', 'entitlement' and 'conjunction'.

Anthony introduces Josephine to the amenities of the small bus he has chartered. It consists of three rooms: A bedroom with office in the rear, a galley cum living room in the middle, and another bedroom with office in front. Screen monitors are in every room.

ANTHONY: Most of the time we'll live here. I have made an itinerary that generally allows us to sleep eight hours overnight as Gertrude takes us automatically from one stop to another. The People appreciate frugality.

JOSEPHINE: Gertrude?

Anthony directs her attention to the mannequin sitting in the driver's seat.

ANTHONY: Meet your driver.

JOSEPHINE: Right.

ANTHONY: Yes, I'm kidding. The driver is the bus itself. I've named her Gertrude.

He places his fingers into his shirt, primping ridiculously.

ANTHONY: Gertrude is self-driving. Ours will be one of the first long-distance, independent journeys. That demonstration, in and of itself, will generate interest. The manufacturer is a friend who supports the cause.

16

The next evening Anthony and Josephine settle in for their first trip with Gertrude. They awake the next morning in the parking lot of the University of Georgia football stadium.

Josephine shakes off the travel with a solitary stroll. An old man comes limping toward her. He wears a faded and tattered T-shirt that proclaims 'Sortition -- not Election -- for a Two-Legged Democracy.'

JOSEPHINE: What does that mean?

LIMPING MAN: I don't know. It's an old shirt. Maybe... I think it's about knowing who the enemy is.

JOSEPHINE: Who?

LIMPING MAN: The People.

JOSEPHINE: Oh? Why?

LIMPING MAN: The People don't believe in elections anymore.

JOSEPHINE: Oh.

LIMPING MAN: Not me. No, siree. I'm not signing up. No way.

JOSEPHINE: Why not?

LIMPING MAN: Qualifications. I'm not.

Josephine waits.

LIMPING MAN: Would you?

She walks on.

Anthony wheels himself into a restaurant where Josephine awaits him.

ANTHONY: We should know a little of what each other is going to say.

JOSEPHINE: I suppose.

ANTHONY: I'm going to say that freedom is a constant struggle.

JOSEPHINE: How original.

ANTHONY: Excuse me?

JOSEPHINE: Union organizers always said that when they tried to get us waitresses organized. They failed.

Anthony looks at her funny.

JOSEPHINE: You and I are not 'together' on this. Remember?

ANTHONY: No, we aren't. But a little cooperation, a little preparation...

JOSEPHINE: I'm not along just for the ride.

ANTHONY: Maybe you need reminding. These town hall meetings that we're going to hold... They are aimed at different audiences. Religious fundamentalists, for one. Rich secular skeptics, for another. These groups are still the-powers-that-be.

JOSEPHINE: Is that so? In that case then, I will have only to influence the conservative, anti-socialist, upper 10%.

Josephine gives no ground.

JOSEPHINE: You don't think we have any real power in the Citizen House?

ANTHONY: You saw those know-nothings who wouldn't listen to my proposal. Sure, the Citizen House is a nice idea. But we representatives have spent most of our time just learning where the bathrooms are. Fears that the poor would take over were groundless. Real power remains in the hands of private business.

JOSEPHINE: We'll see about that.

Josephine smiles a deprecation.

JOSEPHINE: Won't we?

Their first town hall meeting is held at the university's Mahler Center. Promotional posters mentioning eugenics and social welfare have insured that the six hundred seats are full. Thanks to the novelty of two sortitionally-chosen legislators with an unusual agenda and arriving on a self-driving bus, the locals have come to see what many of them consider a first-time type of political sideshow.

Anthony orates from his wheelchair. He opens with a slide show of deformed babies.

ANTHONY: I know you don't like to see these photos. 'Long-term care facilities' are full of these babies. Grown up babies.

He clicks through a dozen photos of the unfortunate.

ANTHONY: We warehouse them, hide them away. Little wonder. Released of the burden of their care. Society generally does not want to see them.

A young man arises, shouting.

18

STRIDENT PROTESTER: What? You want to bring back the 'Ugly Laws'?

EARNEST PROTESTER: You want to hide physical disability? Afraid to offend or frighten the able-bodied?

Anthony shouts back.

ANTHONY: No! I want to abolish the existence of those disabilities before they are even conceived!

Strident Protestor holds up and rattles a sign: 'End Lookism!'

EXCITABLE PROTESTER. Even if you manage with genetic modification to make everyone physically...

STRIDENT PROTESTER: You want to make everyone pretty. So-called.

Anthony modulates, turns instructive.

ANTHONY: My dear protestants... The last of the cities repealed the ugly laws in the mid-1970s. I don't want to discriminate against fat people or skinny people or ugly people.

The protestors boo but he persists.

ANTHONY: Or poor people. They, the poor, were the main targets of those Ugly Laws, you know? Street beggars.

That calms them a little.

Anthony gets back to his slides. Without commentary.

Orphanages of deformed children.

Strident Protester breaks the silence.

STRIDENT PROTESTER: Long-term institutionalization of a child is an act of abuse. Cognitive abilities are lowered. Their growth is slowed. Their brain development is abnormal. The damage is lifelong.

ANTHONY: The Citizen House was established in order to end pervasive prejudice against them. By choosing randomly from among the population, the way one looks no longer matters. We have the benefit of the perspective of people who have suffered from lookism. Those people have never had a chance to be elected.

Strident Protester blows a whistle and a whole slew of protesters suddenly march in with snazzy signs: 'Monster-maker!' 'Fascist!' 'Racist Scum!'

Anthony is not without his own supporters. Many of them, in fact. They yell 'Freedom! Freedom! Freedom!'

Anthony tries to settle his advocates.

ANTHONY: Let them march! Let them march!

His people lower their volume. He goes on, despite the ruckus, declaiming.

ANTHONY: Most citizens think my push for eugenics is marginal to their concerns. They think more about wages and salaries. That's all and good. But I'm thinking long term. The future of the human race. Yes, the race. The human. Got it?

STRIDENT PROTESTER: Genetic modification into future generations will be next! There are advances... They call them advances. Such that practically any old Tom-Dick-or-Harry will be able to manipulate their progeny's genes. Once that cat is out of the bag, there is no retrieving where the race, human as you call it, is headed. Unreflective curiosity kills the cat!

The hall erupts into full-scale riot.

ANTHONY'S SUPPORTERS: Freedom through progress! Eugenics for a better Me-and-You!

PROTESTERS: Happiness through security! A universal basic income releases creativity!

The protesters bash each other with their opposing signs. Blood flows. Police throw tear gas.

In the confused melee, Anthony separates himself in order to hand an envelope to an Unidentified Woman.

The hall empties. The crowd splinters and disperses.

Next day Anthony and Josephine are dining in a restaurant.

ANTHONY: What a start for our first town hall.

JOSEPHINE: Where did they get all those signs so quickly?

ANTHONY: And how did they all rise up together?

The television on the wall is full of pundits. Having a field day.

SAGACIOUS PUNDIT: A closer look at these rioters shows a high degree of preparation. I think it was planned.

PUGILISTIC PUNDIT: It's the military-biopharmaceutical-formerly-congressional-complex speaking up for itself.

STATELY PUNDIT: Multinationals operate far and above what the Citizen House can control.

SAGACIOUS PUNDIT: Not totally. The legislators do have access to classified materials. Which makes for a problem since The People complain that the Citizen House acts without transparency, guided by that classified information.

PUGILISTIC PUNDIT: Right, the Citizen House is no longer pure, no longer 'ordinary citizens'. The reps have the time and resources to know more.

SAGACIOUS PUNDIT: Because of that some segments of the population trust them. And other segments respond with apathy.

STATELY PUNDIT: Many people simply don't care anymore. They have no way to decide which particular person... not just which statistically representative person... will carry their ideas forward. Sortition engenders disengagement. The apathetics don't care about the fact that they are, indeed, represented.

PUGILISTIC PUNDIT: Right, they only see distribution by chance. And automatically assume there is no fair representation in it.

SAGACIOUS PUNDIT: Granted, they know nothing of — or simply do not accept the fact of — the Law of Large Numbers.

STATELY PUNDIT: Too many people don't understand, or ignore, what statistical probability insures.

SAGACIOUS PUNDIT: And they tend to overlook that the Citizen House is statistically-representative only of those who placed themselves in the lottery to serve.

PUGILISTIC PUNDIT: No matter what system is put in place, it must make choices. It must distinguish among competing political influences. That inevitably involves some degree of arbitrariness.

SAGACIOUS PUNDIT: A conundrum, as well as a sine qua non. A certain amount of distrust attends – and thus undermines -- always and everywhere, any and all political arrangements.

After an overnight sleep to New Orleans, Anthony wheels himself out of Gertrude and into the plaza before the cathedral. He looks at the sky, not a cloud in sight. He eats beignets and posts selfies to his followers on social media. He engages with the artists and the tourists.

ANTHONY: We are going to transform America. We're going to get this country back to its self-sufficient roots. Even for those of us descended from slaves, we're going to eliminate all the bureaucracies. We will earn that forty acres. And we'll work the mule.

STARVING ARTIST: Is that so? Freedom for Balthazar?

Starving Artist is working on a very bad portrait of a tourist.

ANTHONY: Nothing else to lose? Yes, the freedom to fail. To suffer the consequences. The only way we make Progress.

STARVING ARTIST: You'll progress, then, with the consequences of that wheelchair?

ANTHONY: Indeed, my friend. We will make you a better artist. You probably don't know that the National Association for the Advancement of Colored People promoted eugenics by hosting 'Better Baby' contests. The proceeds went to its anti-lynching campaign.

STARVING ARTIST: What's that got to do with me? Or with now?

ANTHONY: We can engineer a better eye and a steadier hand for you.

STARVING ARTIST: Really?

Anthony smirks. Superciliously.

Next stop: Indianapolis, Indiana. Gertrude parks itself outside the Motor Speedway.

Anthony visits a biopharmaceutical corporation.

BIOPHARMACEUTICAL CHIEF: Once we've got the general population alerted, we'll be able to get the Citizen House to vote for the bill we want. Even though the pressure of electoral fright is no longer at play – and we can no longer buy our way in -- our advocating will be supported by the push of peer pressure, of ideological status, of friendships, of taboos, of personal interests.

BIOPHARM PUBLICIST: Whatever the outcome of any proposal that requires voting… it's always in our favor since we control the advertising and news media. So much for the 'statistically-representative' force of The People'.

22

BIOPHARM CHIEF: With social media we can do all kinds of juju. We've got our own organs. Hack-a-thon here, flood-the-space there. Disinform, reform, plunder. Set the agenda.

BIOPHARM PUBLICIST: Some independent outlets may still make trouble. But even bad news forces attention to our message.

BIOPHARM CHIEF: As far as those who berate consumer choice for being a determinant… As if a designer baby has choice!

BIOPHARM PUBLICIST: A baby, biologically determined through germ-line genetic engineering, would no more have 'choice' than a Hindu born as an Untouchable.

BIOPHARM CHIEF: Moral concerns may limit, but certainly do not prohibit, germ-line engineering.

Next day, Anthony and Josephine decide to hit the road for a day trip. At an interstate rest area they picnic.

ANTHONY: Nice, to take our time, a bit of a break, moseying north up along the Mississippi.

JOSEPHINE: So far so good. I'm enjoying the travel.

ANTHONY: We've had our first half-year now in the Citizen House. It hasn't been the great radical experiment that proponents predicted. But neither has it been as incompetently detrimental to the republic as nay-sayers warned.

JOSEPHINE: Most people think they are smarter than 90% of the population. Kind of ridiculous, but a matter of fact.

ANTHONY: Which leads to the perception, therefore, that 90% of the Citizen House is less smart than ordinary citizens.

JOSEPHINE: And that is why, even though it might be said that the former Powers-That-Be are now The-People-Themselves, the former power barons still have a lot of it. Power, that is. Perceptions matter.

Next day in Hannibal, Missouri. Another town hall meeting. Anthony visits Mark Twain's Home and, feeling out of sorts, decides to sit this one out.

Josephine shows photos of impoverished farm workers. The audience gives her its rapt attention.

JOSEPHINE: I don't know about you all, but I haven't exactly had it easy. That's despite the fact that I've worked hard all my life and my people have, too. We aren't asking for a free ride, just basic support. That's why I am proposing a Universal Basic Income. Call it UBI. U-B-I.

Her supporters show their signs: 'Happiness = All in this Together'.

The meeting ends with a hundred-strong group hug.

Newspaper headlines blare 'Happiness vs. Freedom?'
Twitter messages fly: 'Give me Progress or Give me Security?'

Josephine and Anthony relax in Gertrude's galley, watching a screen.

Talking heads are at it full steam.

SAGACIOUS PUNDIT: The People are not going to rally behind excessively egalitarian causes.

STATELY PUNDIT: Next thing you know, Josephine will be going for the Mini-Maxi Plan. Limits on income, top and bottom. Ceiling and floor. Even worse than UBI.

PUGILISTIC PUNDIT: Extreme egalitarianism is at odds with liberty. I mean, corporations are people, too. Does she mean to guillotine all productive individuals?

SAGACIOUS PUNDIT: Maybe they wouldn't be capital for the guillotine if they demonstrated some corporate responsibility. They need to acknowledge their taxpayer subsidies. Big time!

STATELY PUNDIT: Aren't you the roaring individualist! Next time you need a cop, call an individualist.

PUGILISTIC PUNDIT: Same thing with political parties. Pretend to be non-partisan, why don't you?

STATELY PUNDIT: The driving force for the employ of sortition… To break up factions.

SAGACIOUS PUNDIT: Government by Do-It-Yourselfers!

STATELY PUNDIT: It's about emotions, not intellect. Partisanship delivers a deep sense of belonging.

SAGACIOUS PUNDIT: As if we don't need to acknowledge it. Fascism is dictatorship of the consensual middle!

The moderator interrupts to run a news clip showing focus groups sprouting up everywhere. They discuss questions like 'What values are our service people protecting?' 'Can we have better living through biogenetics?' 'Is it the end of liberty in A Brave New World?'

Clip concluded, back to the opinionators.

PUGILISTIC PUNDIT: Those who died for the right to vote were actually dying for the right to representation. They were bamboozled to think that voting would get them there.

SAGACIOUS PUNDIT: Meaningful nationwide democracy only arrived at a national level in 1906, when Finland became the first country, in 1906, to abolish race and gender requirements for voting and for serving in government.

Josephine turns away from the TV.

JOSEPHINE: Finland? I thought the United States led in all matters and manners of democracy.

ANTHONY: Oh you naïf.

Josephine removes a shoe and throws it at him.

Back in Indianapolis at the biopharmaceutical headquarters, the Chair of the Board heads a meeting. Seated in Gertrude, Anthony attends as a videoconference guest.

BIOPHARM CHAIR: We've got to support, Anthony. At least a significant percentage of The People believe in the superiority of science.

He power-points a chart onto the wall headed 'What The People Believe'. The word 'cloning' stands out.

ANTHONY: We shouldn't be talking about cloning humans. True, we want more research to improve somatic cell nuclear transfer. But we need only ban reproductive cloning, not the therapeutic. Our reasoning has nothing to do with religious dogma. It is rather about internationally-derived, ethical, secular law.

BIOPHARM CHAIR: Most people would give an arm and a leg — to say nothing of enhanced DNA — to turn their own children into super-people.

ANTHONY: The problem is with those who are constrained by books called divine. Written more than a thousand years ago.

BIOPHARM CHAIR: Our lobbyists have to face those know-nothings in the Citizen House.

Another board member dares to speak up.

BIOPHARM BOARD: And those nabobs making 90% of the median household income. $145,000 a year! So they can deliberate. I don't care if it is less than the old Congress paid themselves.

BIOPHARM CHAIR: Ah, stop your complaining. Everybody, stand up.

He arises. As does everyone else.

BIOPHARM CHAIR: We don't have all day. Clocks aren't made just for ticking. It's a stand-up meeting from here on.

An ad man takes over the meeting to display evocative video poems that subtly undermine any positive perceptions of competence in the Citizen House.

BIOPHARM BOARD : I wonder if we really want to move in this direction? Hasn't it been said often enough that these lottocratic legislators are still stumbling around? Even with three year terms they are still going to be learning basic rules and protocols.

BIOPHARM PUBLICIST: You really do need to know something to pass legislation.

BIOPHARM BOARD: Their professional staffs and the agencies, the departments, all the executive, not least the president herself... All are gaining power.

Anthony interrupts with a wave of his hand.

ANTHONY: Just a minute now.

BIOPHARM CHAIR: I've got a grandfather clock in my office. The pendulum is swinging. Anybody getting tired from standing?

Anthony twitches, goes on.

ANTHONY: I rely on professional friends, advisors and organizations. Like most of the Citizen House, our staff choices are quality people. Some are even former politicos.

BIOPHARM PUBLICIST: The ads are needed anyway. It's just up to this board to decide where to aim them.

26

BIOPHARM BOARD: There are other ways. We've got a plan for Josephine to show up in a little news story that she isn't quite yet aware of.

Jolly good guffaws all around.

BIOPHARM PUBLICIST: She won't know what hit her.

The Chairman flops back into his chair. Meeting adjourned.

In locales countrywide, billboards and posters of conflicting sentiments festoon – and sermons of wide variance grace -- churches, synagogues, mosques and temples. Universities hold teach-ins, some of which are boycotted by students and some of which are prevented by administrative fiat from proceeding at all.

Some succumb to group-think and believe whatever conspiracy theory satisfies. Some rely on certifiable experts, others on glib charlatans.

Debates are authentic. Unpolished. Awkward. Crude.

The whole thing looks like what it is – the untidy mess of an untrammeled democracy.

In a newsroom, editors deliberate over two versions of a political cartoon. The drawing is the same but the captions are different.

A donkey stands equidistant between two enticing piles of hay. Stuck there, indecisive. Likely to die there. Stuck in the middle.

In one version, the caption under one pile of hay reads 'Happiness'. Under the other pile of hay, 'Freedom'.

In the other version, the captions are 'Equality' and 'Progress'.

They wake from an overnight ride, pulling into Fargo, North Dakota.

Josephine takes a morning walk, passing under the landmark 'Fargo' theater marquee. A little farther on she contemplates a billboard, an ad for the military, 'Protecting Freedom and Insuring Equality'.

A woman approaches Josephine.

UNIDENTIFIED WOMAN: I know you. I saw you on TV the other night.

Josephine is polite. Nods.

UNIDENTIFIED WOMAN: You're right about guaranteeing that everyone should have the basic means to support themselves. But unless you seriously cut the military budget, you can't support it.

JOSEPHINE: Yes, I know.

UNIDENTIFIED WOMAN: There is a bill about to enter the pipeline. The Abolition of War bill. Did you know? Will you sign on?

JOSEPHINE: What?

UNIDENTIFIED WOMAN: Sounds nuts, right? War has been with us forever. It's human nature.

JOSEPHINE: Maybe.

UNIDENTIFIED WOMAN: OK so the backers are crazy idealists. They never would have made it into the Congress except for sortition. They're the kind of fringe folk that the anti-sortitionists lamented.

JOSEPHINE: And?

UNIDENTIFIED WOMAN: Just like every legislator in the Citizen House – just like you -- they have access to professional staff. Lawyers and military experts are helping them fashion effective legislation.

Josephine remains wary.

UNIDENTIFED WOMAN: They actually have a plan beyond simply abolishing war. Civilian-Based Defense. Want to hear more?

JOSEPHINE: Let me play the politician. I will… take it under consideration.

She accepts the Unidentified Woman's invitation into a diner.

At town hall meetings around the nation, riots erupt between the libertarians and the egalitarians, spilling into the streets. The sides are equally balanced.

Anthony and Josephine egg on their supporters by encouraging them to undercut each other.

The protesters fly every which way.

28

STRIDENT PROTESTER: We are disenfranchised. We can't even make a little electoral tick.

EARNEST PROTESTER: The just-like-us mantra is belied by the fact that the Citizen House passed a budget that, if there had been an online referendum, would have been defeated.

STRIDENT PROTESTER: Deficit spending, pah! We-The-People would never have supported such outlandishness.

EARNEST PROTESTER: The Citizen House is no longer even close to being statistically-representative. If it ever was. Now that they are privy to state secrets, they cannot be just-like-us.

An opposing protester stands up.

EXCITABLE PROTESTER: What did you expect? What would you have done when you had to vote, for instance, on the environmental treaty? You know nothing about that. But the representatives in the Citizen House have had the time to learn. Would you rather have a referendum by the uninformed masses? Using online voting? You know where that would lead!

That shuts the other up.

STRIDENT PROTESTER: The representatives are accountable to no one and some of them are taking huge gifts. Those big-time lobbyists can buy whomever they want.

EXCITABLE PROTESTER: I want the freedom to create super babies.

HANGER-ON PROTESTER: That threatens my happiness and wellbeing.

OFF-THE-WALL PROTESTER: The Universal Basic Income threatens my liberty.

GOTTA-SAY-SOMETHING PROTESTER: Something that you get for nothing is worth that much!

STRIDENT PROTESTER: And if it's worth nothing, who will pay to guard our freedom?

EXCITABLE PROTESTER: There are the courts.

STRIDENT PROTESTER: What have they got?

EXCITABLE PROTESTER: Sanctions.

EARNEST PROTESTER: Enforceable by whom?

EXCITABLE PROTESTER: Unh… the marshals.

EARNEST PROTESTER: Is that all?

HANGER-ON PROTESTER: That's not much.

EXCITABLE PROTESTER: Well then, by popular acceptance, by common law.

EARNEST PROTESTER: Is that enough?

EXCITABLE PROTESTER: That's a lot.

EARNEST PROTESTER: Oh, is it?

And thus the confabulations proceed. Tangents and side tracks and non sequitors, all.

Inside Gertrude, Josephine and Anthony watch a talk show.

SAGACIOUS PUNDIT: Polls show the populace split down the middle.

PUGILISTIC PUNDIT: On the one hand people are disengaging since they no longer vote for their legislators.

STATELY PUNDIT: Indeed, voting every four years for the President, and every six for the Senate has always failed to generate sustained enthusiasm.

PUGILISTIC PUNDIT: But on the other hand sortition gives more voice than ever because nearly everyone can point to a representative who is closer in spirit and demeanor and viewpoint than any of the old legislative body every did.

SAGACIOUS PUNDIT: Let's admit that we intellectuals and journalists can't swallow our pride. We no longer have the outsize influence we previously had.

PUGILISTIC PUNDIT: There is no accountability with these randomly-selected nobodies who sit in the Citizen House. The loud mouths take over. Whatever their favorite cause is, they bicker and nit-pick. Gun control, socialized medicine, the end of mandatory seat belt usage. It's cacophony!

SAGACIOUS PUNDIT: It was a wanton abrogation of responsibility by the politicians of the old electoral system when they decided to defer to The People. They seem to have forgotten that 'authority' contains within it 'authorship'.

PUGILISTIC PUNDIT: It was that jejune slogan 'Question Authority' that got us here.

STATELY PUNDIT: Half of the populace is apathetic. Freedom is lost gradually by an uninterested, uninformed, and uninvolved people.

SAGACIOUS PUNDIT: Some of these people are agents provocateur. Sources name them as part of the organization called 'Lobak'.

PUGILISTIC PUNDIT: The Citizen House is filled with wimps. Incapable of firm decisions.

STATELY PUNDIT: They waffle like flags in the wind.

SAGACIOUS PUNDIT: Even so, the middle holds.

PUGILISTIC PUNDIT: Give me a break. 'Middle', as in… centrist, namby-pamby, feckless.

SAGACIOUS PUNDIT: Following the loudest wheel that squeaks!

PUGILISTIC PUNDIT: Anthony, that trust fund baby… he might do better if he stopped oiling his wheelchair.

SAGACIOUS PUNDIT: The issues raised are too many, too dispersed.

PUGILISTIC PUNDIT: Protection for whistleblowers.

SAGACIOUS PUNDIT: Prosecution for whistleblowers.

STATELY PUNDIT: Privatizing the internet.

PUGILISTIC PUNDIT: Concealed weapons without permits.

SAGACIOUS PUNDIT: Without a steadier compass we are susceptible to a leader or group with more discipline than all-the-people all-the-time.

STATELY PUNDIT: It's the classic case of Buridan's Ass.
He shows the cartoon of the indecisive donkey.

STATELY PUNDIT: Put it this way. If Happiness tries to sashay with Freedom, Freedom will dance, out of control, calling itself Progress. If Progress then picks up the hand of Security, Freedom will face having to two-step with Equality. Not something Freedom would want to be constrained to do. So each cancels the other.

SAGACIOUS PUNDIT: Maybe a bit of randomness would break them out of their tautological whirl. Say, flip a coin. That will do it.
Josephine harumps. Anthony does, too.

Anthony and Josephine stand on the stage of a town hall meeting in Bozeman, Montana. The place is almost empty.

31

ANTHONY: What is it with this sudden onset of apathy?

JOSEPHINE: It seems that some places are fully apathetic, others fully engaged.

ANTHONY: And some split right down the middle. But how are we going to get anywhere in a place like this if we can't raise any interest?

JOSEPHINE: Maybe if we stopped undercutting each other, we might get somewhere.

ANTHONY: I don't undercut you.

JOSEPHINE: Oh yeah?

ANTHONY: You want people to get more than they deserve.

JOSEPHINE: You want to make people more than they are.

ANTHONY: Lobak has all the expertise, all the smart ones. Why do you think The People know any better than the experts?

JOSEPHINE: The People do. As a hive. It's proven. It's innate. It's why we've got seven billion people on this planet. Humans are the planet's great success. Because they put their minds together. Because, fundamentally, people cooperate.

She looks him in the eye.

JOSEPHINE: And I think Lobak isn't who you think they are.

Both irritated and flustered, they take to the stage before the sparse crowd. Huffing and puffing each their story, they turn their backs on each other. Blowing each other's house down.

Next day, outside of Bozeman, Anthony and Josephine walk around the living room of a ranch house in sight of Sacagawea Peak of the Wallowa Mountains. Friends are helping them set up a small birthday party for Anthony.

ANTHONY: There's more itinerary.

JOSEPHINE: Right.

ANTHONY: Drive on, make your points.

JOSEPHINE: It's your birthday party, for god's sake. Can't you let it go and just enjoy?

ANTHONY: Your advocacy UBI is embarrassing.

JOSEPHINE: I know what you think. Along with all the other people at our last town hall where you belittled me.

ANTHONY: You'd think your Hosts would have put you up to something smarter than that.

JOSEPHINE: Oh, really? In some countries UBI has eliminated poverty.

ANTHONY: Sure, Josephine, your left-wing ideologues like unearned redistribution. There are even some on the right... I would call them misguided... who think that UBI would result in a less meddlesome state.

JOSEPHINE: Sure, why not? If all the bureaucrats for all the multiple social welfare programs were eliminated, and we just gave the money directly to The People, we'd have more than enough to fund the outlay. The redistributive outlay. Right. So there!

Anthony humpfs.

JOSEPHINE: That old idea of… not giving a fish, but teaching how to fish... it neglects mentioning that you need a fishing rod to implement what you've learned. UBI handles that.

She's on a roll.

JOSEPHINE: And also, by the way... mechanization, robots, automation, communications... Here we are, travelling thanks to driverless Gertrude. You can't ask people to get a job when there are none. UBI is the way to prevent social discord and upheaval by preventing the income gap from widening even further.

ANTHONY: Right, dream on.

JOSEPHINE: I will dream on. Towards the emancipatory effects of UBI. As it is, the poor's liberty has no value. Speaking of libertarian.

ANTHONY: A free ride for everybody.

JOSEPHINE: Correction. A free lunch.

The doorbell rings. The first guest arrives, the mayor of Bozeman. They shut up.

Josephine has forgotten to sign the birthday card she has for Anthony. She scribbles fast and hands it to him. He opens the card: 'Haqqy Brthbay, Antouy'.

Anthony gives her a hug. A hug without condescension.

Slightly embarrassed, Josephine moves on to the cake. Cuts it.

JOSEPHINE: See?

She signals Anthony to take a piece.

JOSEPHINE: One of us cuts, the other gets first choice.

ANTHONY: Oh, so it's that easy to resolve our differences?

JOSEPHINE: Duh. Like now you get it?

ANTHONY: Let us say that, at this moment, fraught but transparently a moment at the fulcrum... We have come to the place where we see... 'A Way Forward'. Let us memorialize it. Acronymize it. The A-W-F. A Way Forward. Yes, it's the AWF.

JOSEPHINE: Awf!

ANTHONY: Awf!

They shake on it.

It looks like everything is going to work out hunky dory.

They take a couple of days riding across the top of the country, going over the northern Rockies and up the Cascades during the day. Then into the urban conglomeration of Seattle, Washington.

Josephine remains on Gertrude while Anthony goes to observe a protest march going on downtown.

Some of the marchers are shouting 'Down with the Citizen House!' Others carry signs that cover the waterfront of causes and opinions: 'Control Back to The People!' 'Incarceration for all drunk drivers!' 'Legalize all drugs!' 'Stop drug legalization!' 'Reform the Bankruptcy Law'. 'Lower taxes'. 'Protect health care'. Et cetera.

Passersby on the sidewalks yawn and ignore them.

Back at Gertrude, Josephine answers a knock on the door. The Unidentified Woman invites herself onboard and takes a place opposite Josephine at a table. She wastes no time.

UNIDENTIFIED WOMAN: We want you to join our faction to abolish war.

JOSEPHINE: Put it in writing.

The Unidentified Woman scribbles quickly.

Josephine looks at it: 'Adoltiou of Mar is The Nxet Big Thiug'.

JOSEPHINE: You, too?

The Woman hesitates, embarrassed.

UNIDENTIFIED WOMAN: Yes.

JOSEPHINE: Yes.

34

UNIDENTIFIED WOMAN: The abolition of war requires that we offer an alternative. Did you know that for a couple hundred years the Japanese defended their country without resort to firearms? They had plenty of high-quality rifles, but they didn't use them. The reason wasn't pacifism. It was culture and class.

JOSEPHINE: How?

UNIDENTIFIED WOMAN: The samurai didn't want the commoners to equalize them. They were protecting their status and their livelihood. As private security guards. Or contract killers. Depending upon what side of the sword you were on.

JOSEPHINE: Is that so?

UNIDENTIFIED WOMAN: Yes, and it wasn't just internally. They constructed fake forts on the coasts, whole Hollywood-quality mock-ups. A half mile of cloth painted with formidable weapons. Known as the Tokugawa Defense.

JOSEPHINE: Really?

UNIDENTIFIED WOMAN: Yes, really. And unarmed defense strategies have evolved since then. We want to hold large-scale educational events to teach The People C-B-D, Civilian Based Defense. It's not a radical idea. It requires large-scale simulations to prepare people to engage in nonviolent obstruction against any invader. But, tell you what, let me take you to meet my compatriots.

As they walk out Josephine sees a poster advertising 'War Is a Racket!' by a smiling General Smedley Butler. An over-earnest lady tries to hand them a flyer, 'Support UBI!' But they decline.

Josephine apologizes.

JOSEPHINE: You'll have to excuse my more enthusiastic supporters.

The Unidentified Woman has a Ferrari 275. Josephine notices the bobblehead Thomas Jefferson on the dash board.

UNIDENTIFIED WOMAN: It was a gift. I'm not sure why I've still got it. The old slaveholder. The 'all men are equal' guy. Conflicted over that.

They drive off.

In the middle of the drive the Unidentified Woman slumps over, barely able to steer. The woman is breathing heavily. 'Heart attack' she gasps. She manages to pull over. Josephine jumps behind the wheel and floors the pedal, careening wildly in traffic, aiming for the nearest hospital. Her driving is so extreme that passers-by whip out their smartphones to capture her travel.

At the hospital an Emergency Medical Team swiftly removes the Unidentified Woman from the car and whisks her into an ambulance.

JOSEPHINE: But aren't you going to take her into this hospital?

EMT: We're filled up here. We'll stabilize her on the way to a place that specializes.

The ambulance speeds off, leaving Josephine behind.

Later in the day, Anthony, a man known only as 'Lobak #1', and slew of reporters file through the obligatory security investigation into an unnamed building. Inside they pass a sign 'Bioengineering for a Better Future'. A man in a lab coat leads the group deep into the building.

LAB COAT: Those who oppose what we are doing claim that our crime is, essentially, that we are killing our future selves. I would rather say that we are not killing anything. We are simply altering our progeny's future. Our otherwise imperfect selves.

SNOOPY REPORTER: Not throwing the baby out with the bathwater?

LAB COAT: Merely replacing one future for another.

Questions bubble.

SNIPPY REPORTER: What about the religious people?

SNAPPY REPORTER: Is this the way to banish Parkinson's or Tay-Sachs disease?

One directs a question to Anthony.

SNOOPY REPORTER: Is this what you and your group mean when they support de-regulation?

SNIPPY REPORTER: How do you get enough votes in the Citizen House to pass that de-regulation? Are you going to promote statuary regulations to the National Institute of Health or the FDA? Won't that go against your de-regulatory policies?

SNOOPY REPORTER: What are you going to offer those backbenchers who don't give a damn, one way the other, about this stuff? What kind of quid for the quo — of a vote? Inside the Citizen House you still do balloting. So what do you have to give?

36

Anthony stops the barrage.

ANTHONY: For one thing, we can suggest that abortions of fetuses afflicted with a prenatal disease will be no more. A lot of the opposition will be assuaged by that. Furthermore, let's be real. The very question about whether this eugenic impulse should exist is moot.

LAB COAT: He's right. The strides in genetic engineering should not be called eugenics.

SNAPPY REPORTER: What do you mean?

LAB COAT: No one disagrees that we want ourselves and our children to be healthy, intelligent, and fit. There aren't any dictatorial top-down directives. Nor even is there some overarching desire to improve the whole species. No, it's simply about individuals making free choices about their progeny.

REPORTERS: Be that as it may, there are plenty of people who are morally opposed to playing God. They disagree with those who would permit only the parents to have the right to genetically modify their offspring. They go further and say that every fetus has a right to remain genetically unmodified. They want a total ban.

LAB COAT: We need to put aside our self-righteous Euro-American ideological bias. If we don't, you can be sure that others have no such compunctions. If we don't engage, we're only going to become less and less competitive with those who self-improve. It isn't too much to forecast, in fact, that those who refuse to progress will, over time, become enslaved to their betters. It's really quite simple. Genetic engineering is just another technique of enhancement. Compare it to cosmetic surgery. Or even dieting, exercise, education.

REPORTERS: OK, let's say what you predict is accurate. If we de-regulate these emerging reprogenetic technologies won't that mean that only those with the greatest financial resources would be able to, as you say, progress? Once more the gap between rich and poor will be exacerbated by creating a genetic divide.

A reporter snickers.

SNOOPY REPORTER: Society will divide into genetic nobility and the un-enhanced.

SNAPPY REPORTER: Let's stop beating around the bush. We're talking about euthanasia, eventually.

Snappy Reporter enforces his point by slicing his neck with his finger.

LAB COAT: Do I need to remind you that it was the Progressive Era that brought euthanasia to the fore? In 1907, Indiana passed the first eugenics-based compulsory sterilization law in the world. It wasn't the Nazis. At Nuremberg the Nazi defense established that they got the idea from California. It was there in California, before the Nazis came to power, that a respected American institution proposed building gas chambers. To cleanse society of the genetically unfit. It turned out that Americans weren't quite ready for that then. But a little later the Germans were.

SNOOPY REPORTER: Not that eugenic euthanasia wasn't practiced in the U.S. Some mental institutions fed milk infected with tuberculosis to its incoming patients. The good doctors reasoned that the genetically fit would show their superior resistance. Indeed, only a little more than one-third of them died.

ANTHONY: So, reporters, are you going to write a history of your own concoction? Or will you write the story of All-The-People who want this technology?

SNAPPY REPORTER: The People may want a lot of things. Capital punishment, for instance. Or declaring war on a some 'enemy' because a bunch of thugs decide to start a rumble. Which turns into a war. Which engenders genocide. Which goes nuclear. And on to omnicide.

ANTHONY: You don't sound like a reporter. You sound like an ideologue.

SNOOPY REPORTER: Besides all the stuff we've talked about here, there is the issue of genetic diversity. Once everybody begins to choose some culturally-accepted improvement, there will be a degradation of the gene pool. This is seen in numerous studies of isolated island populations. Due to hyper-specialization and a self-selected monopolization, the result is extinction. Those 'improvements' will die en masse, due to increased vulnerability to disease, reduced ability to adapt to environmental change, and other factors both known and unknown. The elimination of traits deemed undesirable would, by definition, reduce genetic diversity.

LAB COAT: Ah, maybe so. Maybe so. Through technology we become as angels. There's no putting the genie back in the bottle. And so, as genies -- or angels -- we might as well get good at it.

SNAPPY REPORTER: And if, maybe, just maybe, you don't measure up to angelic standards?

LAB COAT: There are international treaties. Such as the Cartagena Protocol on Biosafety which protects against the risks.

That brings a laugh from the reporters.

SNAPPY REPORTER: Sure, sure. That's going to stop some pimply-faced hacker, sitting in his parent's basement, from preventing him...

The man from Lobak pulls Anthony aside and whispers in his ear.

LOBAK #1: We are at your back, Tony, my boy. That you know. But...

Lobak #1 lets it hang.

LOBAK #1: ... some of us more than others.

Anthony snaps around.

ANTHONY: Who told you to call me that? 'Tony'?

LOBAK #1: We all do, Tony. That's what you are, right?

Lobak #1 raises his eyebrow, high-class.

Anthony lets it drop.

ANTHONY: At my back, hunh? Some more than others?

LOBAK #1: We've got a rogue faction out there. They have trouble taking orders from headquarters.

He smiles crookedly.

LOBAK #1: Can you imagine that?

ANTHONY: What's their motive?

LOBAK #1: Oh, nothing much. They call it Self-Replicating Singularity.

ANTHONY: Terminator stuff?

LOBAK #1: I guess so, yeah. They only want to rule the world.

Leaving in mid-afternoon in order to glimpse the backside of Yellowstone, Gertrude goes on to drive them overnight to St. George, Utah.

JOSEPHINE: This place received the most radioactive fallout from the atmospheric nuclear tests of the 1950's.

ANTHONY: I wonder if that has any political effect, so long now after?

JOSEPHINE: The downwinders received compensation. For cancer. Odd, to be in such a place...

ANTHONY: Not really. Testing had to be somewhere.

That evening they hold a town hall meeting in an outdoor concert venue cradled between two cliffs of red rimrock. Anthony gives a wink and a nod to a couple of shady looking characters, shills from Lobak.

AUDIENCE: Generations of our forebears died for the right to vote. Some of us still question sortition.

JOSEPHINE: Sortition makes the actuality of that vote even stronger. It makes sure that everyone is represented.

AUDIENCE: Whatever happened to the goal of participatory democracy?

ANTHONY: That is what we have as a republic. Which is to say, a representative democracy. True, we were not elected. But, as they say: 'We is You'. And 'You is Us'.

JOSEPHINE: Most people prefer a legitimating-democracy. Not a participatory-democracy. Most people aren't that excited about voting on everything all the time. That was true before the Citizen House and it's still true now.

AUDIENCE: You are right, Ms. Josephine, about that legitimating democracy. I really, personally, don't much care what you all do. As long as there is someone who is enough like me in the legislature, then I feel represented.

AUDIENCE: I feel the same way. I like the lottery for a lot of things. It's as fair as can be. And it allows me to be apathetic!

JOSEPHINE: There can be a reasonable apathy for politics. Which is not the same as political apathy.

A protester breaks in.

PLEADING PROTESTER: Cleverly stated. But get real! Legitimacy relies on two factors. First, on performance. Second, on the extent to which the representatives reflect underlying values and norms. Most of us don't much care about the eugenics stuff. We are concerned about jobs, taxes, welfare and health care.

40

INDIGNANT PROTESTER: Most of us don't want a handout with UBI. We want the sense of pride that comes with honest work for an honest wage.

The two protesters raise signs: 'RepealTheLot.org'

PLEADING PROTESTER: Back to a Congress that represents voters! Not deadbeats!

INDIGNANT PROTESTER: Repeal the Amendment that created the Citizen House!

The two Lobak Shills look at each other.

SHADY SHILL: Who the hell are those two?

SHADIER SHILL: Loose cannons. Taking our line, but jumping the gun.

SHADY SHILL: Maybe they'll provide some cover. A diversion. Media likes the outliers.

SHADIER SHILL: They aren't going to get anywhere.

SHADY SHILL: Never know how these things can take off sometimes.

Tweets fly from smartphones: 'No accountability from The Citizen House. Repeal!'

Arising mysteriously all at once, hard copy petitions circulate to abolish the Citizen House. The meeting grinds to a milling, indefinite conclusion.

Josephine and Anthony hash it out as Gertrude barrels through the night.

ANTHONY: The success of sortition at the state level only worked when there was geographical closeness. Municipalities and state houses.

JOSEPHINE: But at the national level, that proximity is lost. Plus you've got these rumors of corruption.

ANTHONY: It's similar to what happened with the 18th Amendment. First a great wave of enthusiasm to eliminate drunkenness. Then organized crime took over and everybody sobered up. With sortition, the impulse was to clean up the oligarchy inevitably created by elections. We got rid of the politicians. And here we are.

He takes a breath.

ANTHONY: And now… buyers remorse!

JOSEPHINE: In the old Congress there was a great unevenness of representation. In comparison, for example, the Swiss legislature only has 6% of its legislators are lawyers. Half of the old U.S. Congress were lawyers.

ANTHONY: And once elected, they practically had a sinecure. They had to really screw up. Incumbents ruled!

JOSEPHINE: On the other hand, Anthony, a three year term doesn't give us much time to know what's up. The staggering of newcomers — one-third every year — that helps. But still, I still wonder if the one-term limit might end in disaster?

Heading south, they stop by Lava Beds National Monument and the memorial to the only World War Two fatalities on the North American continent -- six victims of Japanese fire balloon.
They arrive in Alturas, California.

JOSEPHINE: I admit, Anthony, that I am gratefully beholden to you for inviting me on this trip. You've made room for my advocacy of UBI. I'm sorry for you... that more people seem interested in their income than in their genes.

Anthony gulps, a tight smile, swallowing the duplicity of his inviting her.

JOSEPHINE: But Anthony, I don't understand how you can hold with supremacist views. Your friends in Lobak are mongering fear, saying that implementation of UBI requires fascist domination. And that it would be creating equality at the expense of competence. Do you believe that?

Anthony slips a video into the player. It's a sneering right-wing announcer.

ANNOUNCER: Libertarianism is the positive view, supporting the individual. Anarchism is the negative view, eliminating state power. Fascism claims to be a form of benevolent dictatorship. The malevolent form is when that dictatorship is led by only one person. The good form of fascism is when the dictatorship is led by the consent of the middle. For all those who want to remain apolitical, who want merely a legitimating democracy, a benevolent dictatorship is the most desirable.

Anthony stops the video.

42

ANTHONY: Is that what you want? With your UBI, all individuals will be relieved of scrapping for their livelihood. So why not turn it all over to a benevolent dictatorship? That's what your UBI leads to.

He curls his lip.

ANTHONY: Nothing supremacist about that, is there?

It is a 12 hour ride to San Diego, most of it during the day to see the scenery of the eastern Sierra Nevada.

Next day at a hotel conference room, Anthony, Lobak #1 and Lobak #2 meet.

LOBAK #1: Things are going well, Tony boy. The repeal campaign is taking off. We're going to blast this wide open. Check out this ad.

He shows him a mock-up billboard: 'All For One, One For All.'

Lobak #2 unfurls her long hair and flounces.

LOBAK #2: It promotes eugenics on the basis of making all people productive and competitive.

LOBAK #1: And take a look at this man-on-the-street.

He shows him a poster of a homeless woman carrying a sign: 'Aimless Wandering'. Then he opens his smartphone to a video of a worker sweeping a street.

STREET SWEEPER: Competition does not equal merit.

The man speaks confidently. Forcefully.

STREET SWEEPER: Winners of elections prove their ability, meritocratically, to win elections. Random is as random does. Competition exceeds its bounds, just as money does, when applied to relationship.

Lobak #1 lowers his smartphone.

LOBAK #1: Too erudite, that one. No worry, we can edit to make it fit. Besides the word 'random' has morphed from a precise statistical term into an all-purpose phrase that stresses the illogic and coincidence of life.

LOBAK #2: I thought societies that emphasize luck over logic are unlikely to thrive.

LOBAK #1: What's the matter, girl? Haven't drunk the kool aid? We're making most of our money now off the casinos.

Libertarians are for casinos, don't you know? It is the egalitarians who are not.

ANTHONY: Yeah, chewing up poor people with a false promise.

LOBAK #1: Lighten up, man. You don't like that one? Then check out this other.

He lifts up his smartphone.

It is another ad which laments deadlock and apathy. With the Citizen House as exhibit one. The ad calls for implementation of eugenics to improve the lot of the Citizen House.

LOBAK #1: Remember that eugenics does not equate with euthanasia. We are trying to bring out the best in people.

Anthony snickers.

ANTHONY: Wouldn't a natural disaster do a better job of bringing out altruism?

Lobak #1 laughs along.

LOBAK #1: We have no control over natural disasters.

He turns more serious

LOBAK #1: But a war would do nicely.

Anthony squirms, squeamish.

LOBAK #1: Ah, Tony my boy. Are those little leftover scruples? My father told me. He was there at 'Balthazar'. Your mother's betrayal…

Anthony blushes but parries by ignoring.

ANTHONY: The repeal campaign seems to have run its course. Yeah, it went viral but now it's leveling. Seems as if there wasn't quite enough umpf.

LOBAK #1: Is that so? Well, one never knows what the tipping point is. Maybe we haven't seen the last of surprises.

LOBAK #2: Eye on the ball, Anthony! Remember Thoreau: 'That government is best which governs least.'

Anthony smiles wanly.

ANTHONY: Oh yeah?

Anthony leaves.

Lobak #1 turns immediately to his subaltern.

LOBAK #1: Start up a whispering campaign against Josephine's UBI. Spread it through religious institutions. Call it socialism. Call it pagan. Say it's enslavement, shackling progress.

44

Lobak #1 licks his fingers and chuckles to himself.
LOBAK #1: Matter of fact, call it 'Sempre ubi sub ubi'.
Lobak #2 scratches her head.
LOBAK #2: Dissing Josephine's shtick?
LOBAK #1: A sophomoric joke. 'Sempre' means 'always'. 'Ubi' means 'where' as in 'Where are you going?' 'Sub' means 'under', like in 'submarine'. 'Where' is a homonym. You know what a homonym is? Something that sounds alike, but has totally different meaning. Like 'where' — where are you going — sounds the same as 'wear', like you wear clothes. You follow?
LOBAK #2: Unh. Yeah.
LOBAK #1: So, put it all together and you've got… 'Sempre' — 'Always'… 'Ubi sub ubi'... Wear underwear!
He laughs hysterically.
Then he flips open his computer tablet to a video clip of Josephine wildly driving the Ferrari 275 through city traffic with the Unidentified Woman beside her.
LOBAK #1: Go talk to the woman. Not to Josephine. You mentioned a 'juicy story'. You'll find one there.
Lobak #2 departs. Lobak #1 makes a call. A Female Voice answers.
LOBAK #1: This boy Anthony. Pitiful. He needs some genetic engineering for himself.
The Female Voice laughs.
LOBAK #1: But we can't have you always going off on your own. This kidnapping idea won't do us any good. Come on in for a talk.
The line goes dead. Lobak #1 immediately receives a text: 'Lobak as you see it'. With an emoji of a chicken. Then immediately, another text: 'Rogues can do better than that.'
Lobak #1 sighs. He returns to the video clip of Josephine in the Ferrari and sinks into contented reverie.

Journalists suck up the ads and relish the gossip. They amplify whatever is a little odd and call it news. In one newspaper editorial room a well-drawn graphic hangs on poster board. Titled: 'The Sphere of Legitimacy'.

DISPUTATIOUS EDITOR: State power is perforce aligned with other forms of power. The state's elitist nature is, thus, unavoidably corrosive to society.

DISQUISITIVE EDITOR: It is, nonetheless, indispensable.

DISPUTATIOUS EDITOR: It can only be reformed. Not destroyed.

DISQUISITIVE EDITOR: To think that political elites can be banished is fanciful. Their role must simply be delimited.

In a penthouse Lobak #1 chuckles as he reads an online op-ed titled 'The Sphere of Legitimacy'.

LOBAK #1: People think it's expensive to send these shills out into the streets, to the town halls. But it's peanuts really. And besides, they have themselves a ball.

He clicks on the accompanying ad. It's for the petrochemical industry: 'America runs on fossil fuels'. It features Josephine swerving through traffic in the Ferrari 275. At the end he clicks on the Twitter icon. It leads to the petition to repeal.

In a sports bar Anthony looks up to the television, playing the ad. This is followed by a news report.

NEWS REPORTER: Now we have the latest wrinkle in the charges of bribery brought against the representative.

Anthony is perplexed.

A MAN ON BARSTOOL: It doesn't matter, does it? How they get in. Power seduces anyone. It's all just too sweet.

BARTENDER: How about it, Mister Representative?

The bartender evidently knows Anthony.

ANTHONY: I don't know about that.

MAN ON BARSTOOL: What, you think they did the old split-the-cake thing? Man, are you naive.

ANTHONY: Maybe I am.

REPORTER ON TV: We find ourselves in this strange situation of apathy and activism.

ANTHONY (to bartender): The repeal may or may not be such a good idea. But the friendships I have... The People I've known for a long time, people who I've grown up with... People I

46

think highly of, maybe they aren't as upstanding as I thought, but they're my friends. Loyalty is everything.

MAN ON BARSTOOL: If this Josephine woman is any example… What balls the petrochemicals have got… to use that undercover video of her in the Ferrari… looks like prima facie evidence of her taking a bribe… I wonder if the Ethics Committee will take it up? And will the FBI investigate and the Department of Justice bring charges? It's a long way to indictment.

Anthony squirms.

ANTHONY: I don't like to think it's going to go in that direction. Josephine may be a piece of work. I often regret having invited her along. But I'd be surprised if she would take a bribe.

BARTENDER: What about campaign finance reform? Eliminate campaign contributions altogether. Fully finance elections. Why not? For the Senate and Presidency right away. And scrap sortition. Get back to elections. But make sure there is no private funding.

ANTHONY: Money is the slipperiest thing there is. Infinitely fungible. There will always be ways to get around.

Inside a ramshackle house a ragtag bunch of self-styled Liberationists, including Unidentified Woman, huddle around a computer screen.

CURLY LIBERATIONIST: We oughta have a name for ourselves.

CRINKLY LIBERATIONIST: Yeah. Some of our so-called buddies in Lobak keep referring to us as The Rogues.

FLAXEN LIBERATIONIST: That's cool. Why not take it on? Call ourselves 'The Rogues.'

UNIDENTIFIED WOMAN: That's good. But make it more exotic. The point is to put up a frightening front. Like my favorite example, the Tokogawa Japanese. Use 'Fusei-sha'. 'The Rogues' in Japanese.

CURLY LIBERATIONIST: Hmm? Well, that's good. Yeah. Exotic. But that's too exotic. And the Japanese are always suspect. Pearl Harbor lingers.

CRINKLY LIBERATIONIST: What about recalling the French Revolution? A bloody mess that was. Everybody loves the

French Revolution. How about Frenchifying it? Call ourselves 'Les Rouges'.

He smiles a dastardly smile.

CRINKLY LIBERATIONIST: Sounds like 'The Rogues'. Make them think we're stupid.

UNIDENTIFIED WOMAN: It means 'The Reds'.

CURLY LIBERATIONIST: Ha! That's good. Confuse the hell out of them.

They all laugh.

LES ROUGES JOYEUX (formerly CURLY LIBERATIONIST): Our Lobak compatriots are lily-livered shrinking violets. All they want is prettier, smarter humans.

LES ROUGES INDISCIPLINE (formerly CRINKLY): Pah! Afraid of moving beyond eugenics.

LES ROUGES JOYEUX: They may think of us as primitive, less well resourced than they. With their biopharmaceutical institutions. With their dinosaurs.

LES ROUGES INDISCIPLINE: We're networked as well as they. And without institutional restraints, we'll see who wins this one.

They laugh heartily again.

Anthony and Josephine ride overnight, east to Las Cruces, New Mexico. Josephine takes an excursion to see the fossil footprints of the 15-foot long, 500 pound Dimetrodon.

Snacking afterwards at a coffee shop, she notices a headline on a newspaper on the counter: 'Report criticizes UBI'. She reads the first paragraph: 'A Nobel Prize winning economist berates a Universal Basic Income.'

Josephine bristles. The waitress comes by. Josephine points to the charts in the newspapers.

JOSEPHINE: Three arguments this Nobel yahoo puts out. First, he says UBI will lead to nobody working and the cost ballooning. Second, he says, employers will stiff their workers, rationalizing that since everyone's basic needs will be covered, wages will be seen as mere gratuities. Third, he opines that there will be widespread moral resistance to being paid without working. He forecasts a cultural backlash.

48

She flops down the paper.
JOSEPHINE: All three arguments are just wrong.
WAITRESS: Well, there is a point in number three.
Josephine is startled that the waitress engages.
WAITRESS: It goes against a fundamental taboo in this capitalist society. Those who decide not to work will be an insult to the moral principal of reciprocity. If you remove the connection between income and contribution, you're just going to make people into parasites.
Josephine smiles.
JOSEPHINE: Well, well! You are one of the populace who is Someone-Just-Like-Me.
She muses, catching herself.
JOSEPHINE: That would be a S-J-L-M.
She blushes.
WAITRESS: Hunh?
JOSEPHINE: I'm a representative in the Citizen House. Acronym hell. It's contagious. S-J-L-M. Someone Just Like Me.
The waitress winks her eye.
WAITRESS: You mean those of us who adhere to defensible disputatious disquisitions?
Josephine acknowledges her. Double. Doppelganger.
JOSEPHINE: Honey, you said it. We all are waitressing our way through this life.
WAITRESS: Community college and a little extra reading on the side.
JOSEPHINE: We need to go a little deeper. Pay attention to our own interests. If we had UBI, would you become a parasite?
WAITRESS: I might take a few more days off.
JOSEPHINE: I wonder how far you'd go, to make UBI real?
WAITRESS: Far.
JOSEPHINE: A hundred years ago a suffragette, Anna Howard Shaw, said to the government: 'You may pick my pocket because you are stronger than I, but I'm not going to turn my pockets wrong-side out for you'.
Josephine hesitates, sips her coffee.
JOSEPHINE: Tax resistance? Risking garnishment of your wages?

The waitress scoffs.
WAITRESS: I'm in. And I've got plenty of friends.

Josephine and Anthony sleep on the overnight ride from Las Cruces to San Antonio, Texas.
Josephine is at the sink in the bathroom at the Alamo. Next to her a woman primps her bouffant.
BOUFFANT: Do you know what it's like to wake up in the morning and not know if you'll have something to eat? Or at least something decently edible to eat? I like pizza, for instance, but my boy... he likes fried chicken. In my town you can't get both at the same place. In my little town. But I'm well fed. I don't know. I read the political stuff. Or my son reads it. He's a civil engineer, keeps River Walk in line. He doesn't believe what this Citizen House is up to. Anyway, we've had enough.
JOSEPHINE: You've heard about the tax resistance movement? For UBI?
BOUFFANT: Word spreads fast online. Yes, we're organizing. This is going to be big. We have set up an escrow account that the I.R.S. can't touch.

At an ATM dispenser outside a bank, two women are waiting in line.
FUSSY WOMAN: UBI isn't going to mean employers will reduce wages.
PRISSY WOMAN: The government isn't going to collapse.
FUSSY WOMAN: Taxes will actually go down.
PRISSY WOMAN: People will be freed to work for the common good. Most people don't like to do nothing but laze around.
FUSSY WOMAN: I'm with Josephine. I'm putting my money in an escrow account.
PRISSY WOMAN: Institute a national sales tax, coupled with UBI. That's the ticket to a really productive society.

In Washington DC at the headquarters of the Internal Revenue Service, officials hold a news conference.
FLUSTERED OFFICIAL: Tax refusal is rising exponentially. We simply don't have the personnel to deal with it.
50

OFFICIOUS OFFICIAL: This isn't only about damage to the government's income stream. It is damage to our sense of justice, of probity, of patriotism.

FLUSTERED OFFICIAL: This traitorous action is being led by a member of the federal legislature!

Back in San Antonio at a bistro on the River Walk, Josephine meets with supporters.

ENTHUSIASTIC SUPPORTER: We also must show that you are sincere, Josephine, about your support of the Abolition of War bill.

FAWNING SUPPORTER: Just because they make outrageous insinuations...

ENTHUSIASTIC: Just because of the incident with the Ferrari...

FAWNING: Your stand on UBI doesn't mean...

ENTHUSIASTIC: And tax resistance!

FAWNING: Wonderful!

ENTHUSIASTIC: No way they can make their smear stick.

FAWNING: Tax resistance goes right along with the Abolition of War bill.

ENTHUSIASTIC: In fact, your vigorous actions in support of the bill will fully clear you.

JOSEPHINE: You're right. I believe in closing the overseas bases. All of them. And using the money here at home to fund UBI.

In Washington a large protest march arrives at the Pentagon and sets up cordons blocking doors, preventing officials and soldiers from entering.

BLUSTERY COP: We can ignore these assholes. Small fry.

SNIDE COP: There is more than one way to skin a cat.

They har-har.

A Newscaster interviews a police commander.

NEWSCASTER: Why aren't you opening up an entrance?

COMMANDER: We've been ordered to avoid provoking a reaction.

NEWSCASTER: You aren't enforcing the law.

COMMANDER: We're preventing a riot. We're peace officers.

NEWSCASTER: Oh.

COMMANDER: It's called defense of democracy.

Anthony and Josephine wake up in Knoxville, Tennessee. A little later Anthony guides a group of his friends past a street fair, the Kuumba Festival.

ANTHONY: 'Kuumba' is Swahili for 'creativity'.

He smiles slyly.

ANTHONY: Didn't think I knew my heritage, did you?

He keeps rolling past the dashiki clad vendors, heading towards an exclusive spa. Inside, Anthony rolls himself over to a large Jacuzzi and lifts himself to join his friends.

ANTHONY: My travel companion is making a bigger splash than we are. We have to do something dramatic.

SALLOW FRIEND: OK, let's jump on the environmental wagon. And, ha-ha, add some 'minority rights' into it.

ROSY FRIEND: Let's occupy the National Parks. They're spread all around the nation. Great Smokey is nearby, start there.

SALLOW FRIEND: Anthony, what about eugenics? What does this have to do with that?

ANTHONY: All publicity is good publicity. And it's clear anyway that survival of the fittest works best when things are stripped down to essentials. Back to the paleo. Or forward to it.

Anthony live-streams himself, standing in old growth forest, exhorting protesters.

ANTHONY: We recognize the right of the original people to these lands! We accept their right of return. Let them re-inhabit their birthright. Welcome them!

From Oklahoma, the Cherokee retrace the Trail of Tears, returning on foot to reclaim eastern Tennessee and western North Carolina. Near Great Smoky Mountain National Park some inhabitants open their homes to the flood.
Others pick up rifles and aim. No one fires. Everyone holds their breath.

52

In several other states, armed men and women take other over national parks. Events turn chaotic.

Gertrude turns back west for an overnight trip to Whiteman Air Force Base, Knob Noster, Missouri. Anthony holds a morning press conference at the decommissioned intercontinental ballistic missile site.

ANTHONY: We libertarians agree with the effort to divest from war industries. We agree with closing foreign bases. We are against acceding to the International Criminal Court. We are for eliminating the nukes since they require such a huge governmental structure to maintain and deploy them. War does not equal defense; it equals imperialism.

SNOOPY REPORTER: Isolationism fosters imperialism!

Anthony pulls out 'War Is a Racket' and flaps it as he paraphrases.

ANTHONY: First. War-making must be made unprofitable. No more profits for the arms manufacturers. Second. To declare war, a referendum limited to those who would risk death on the front lines. Third. Militaries only for self-defense. Operational only within 200 miles of the coasts.

He slams close the book.

ANTHONY: In other words, like Article Nine of the Japanese Constitution. The point is to ensure that war, if fought, can never be one of aggression.

SNOOPY REPORTER: Nor 'humanitarian intervention'? Nor sibling protection?

ANTHONY: Right. No more 'vengeance is mine'.

Josephine stays behind in Gertrude to visit her Hosts via internet video.

HOST WIFE: Way to go, Jo. You've made some strides.

Josephine accepts the compliment but winces at the nickname.

HOST HUSBAND: We commend you, Jo. You have become a social populist in formation. But, Jo, you seem to have forgotten about the larger point, concomitant to UBI.

HOST WIFE: You should be making the point that the country must seek a lower economic level. We should be aiming to move downward, into the mid-range. On par with Peru, Indonesia or South Africa. For global environmental sustainability.

JOSEPHINE: Oi vey.

Host Wife smiles.

JOSEPHINE: That's idealistic, wouldn't you say? And, for you to say it, hypocritical? Are you really willing to be downwardly mobile? To sacrifice your plush lifestyle?

HOST HUSBAND: Isn't it only fair? No longer to be eating up an inordinate amount of the earth's resources?

JOSEPHINE: Some of us never did fit into that camp of 'eating up inordinate resources'. We might rather like to experience it. We never were in the top ten percent. And it's only for our three years in the Citizen House that we'll inhabit that 90th percentile.

HOST WIFE: Jo, you have the right experience and the right attitude. When you leave the legislature, you won't need to waitress again.

JOSEPHINE: What then?

HOST HUSBAND: Lobby for better labor laws. We could fix you up with our former associates.

JOSEPHINE: Not to think about now.

Josephine shrugs and closes the video internet.

In the top floor of a building harboring a casino, Lobak holds a closed door meeting at their Washington headquarters.

LOBAK: We've convinced authorities to make just enough head-on confrontations to keep the protests simmering. But not boiling over. Good thing the House is so contentious.

LOBAK #2: The People are tiring of demands from so many interest groups. Look at all the signs we see at their rallies: 'States' Rights!' 'Federal Oversight!' 'President Must Lead!' 'Down with the Electoral College!' 'Stop Interventionist Judges!' 'Strengthen the Courts!'

LOBAK #1: And a lot of uproar against the park occupiers, the Pentagon protesters and the tax refusers. The formerly apathetic are beginning to takes sides.

LOBAK #3: There are too many factions in the Citizen House. It is just as dysfunctionally deadlocked as the old House of Representatives was.

LOBAK #1: All we need to do is to stoke the anger. We'll shift support to whatever interest group seems to be losing. But not enough to make any of them winners.

The summer is hot. There are small riots and disturbances between and among the various contending sides.

Lobak shills run polls that indicate dissatisfaction mounting against the Citizen House. And movement for a return to elections for the lower house.

A group of representatives of the still-in-recess Citizen House issue a joint statement, posting it online. Anthony and Josephine read it from one of Gertrude's monitors.

JOINT STATEMENT: We are the grandchildren of those who began the Civil Rights Movement. They understood that the rubric of 'citizenship' was one's protection. With the state being the guarantor. They moved us another step towards universal suffrage. Another step on the evolutionary march from the Magna Carta and on beyond the Universal Declaration of Human Rights. As Frederick Douglass is renowned for saying: If there is no struggle there is no progress… Power concedes nothing without a demand. It never did and it never will.

In New York City at the headquarters of a human rights organization, two workers critique the joint statement.

SWEET HUMANITARIAN: Right. A march forward with lots of steps backwards. For instance, when Dred Scott tried to steal himself… The law said he was property.

SOUR HUMANITARIAN: Another irony of history.

SWEET HUMANITARIAN: Slave Scott tried to steal himself.

SOUR HUMANITARIAN: Irony of history. Condemned back into slavery for the crime of stealing oneself.

In the Great Smokey Mountains a passel of Proto-Paleo women and men have set up camps. They hunt wildlife, cook over open campfires, sleep in wickiups. On the way back into 'nature'.

SMILEY PROTO-PALEO: Man, this groundhog's tasty.

SOURPUSS PROTO-PALEO: Too bad the deer have disappeared. I like venison better.

AFFECTLESS PROTO-PALEO: Too many out here going paleo.

One guy is eating a tiny sparrow.

SOURPUSS PROTO-PALEO: Slim pickings.

SMILEY PROTO-PALEO: It's not as much fun as it was before. Who would have thought we could burn through these forests so quickly?

On another ridge bad elements stoke up a meth lab. Some folks are nodding out on heroin.

On another ridge militias, armed with assault weapons, practice techniques of hit-and-run.

Radio silence from Lobak.

Much tut-tutting among the elite. They deem the invasions 'anarchy'. They say that back to the 'state of nature' a la Rousseau validates an inherent lawlessness of 'ordinary citizens'.

Some still hold that the two hundred year displacement of the Cherokee to Oklahoma does qualify as legitimate reclamation of occupied lands.
All of them tend to say the whole endeavor was a wreck easily predicted.

Josephine and Anthony sleep on the overnight trip to the Black Hills of South Dakota. In the morning they pay a visit to the encampment of protesters going paleo. Half are locals, half from elsewhere.

Josephine and Anthony visit the Crazy Horse monument. The happenstance audience there is made up of ragged blue jeans, t-shirts with messages and babies in backpacks. Josephine's plea for UBI finds warm welcome.

At Mount Rushmore, the shirts have collars, pants are pressed and the sandals are moderately heeled. Anthony's case for eugenics generates low-key enthusiasm. Handshakes afterwards.

But at each place, besides speaking in favor of their respective ideas, they each berate the other, teeth gnashing.

Josephine opens her computer tablet to a news report showing a prosecutor holding up the bobblehead Thomas Jefferson that was on the dashboard of the Ferrari 275. The bobblehead concealed a video camera.

JOSEPHINE: See, I told you. It was an obvious set up. I was framed into looking like I was taking a bribe.

She fumes.

JOSEPHINE: I might be nothing but trailer trash but I have principles that would never permit me to take a bribe.

ANTHONY: You've been nothing but a distraction. I should never have invited you. I didn't realize how nutty people can be swayed by a 'gimme'. Your UBI sounds great but it just means ne'er-do-wells will benefit. It saps the entrepreneurial spirit of The People.

JOSEPHINE: If it hadn't been me that pushed for UBI, it would have been someone else who would have.

ANTHONY: I wonder what they had in mind, spending all that time to frame you? For the abolition of war? What are the motives?

JOSEPHINE: Maybe they like war?

ANTHONY: Maybe they like war profiteering. They may be for the abolition of war, but economically there's nothing more profitable than arms sales.

JOSEPHINE: That's extremely short sighted, ignoring all the social costs.

ANTHONY: Maybe so. What matters to me is that they've been supporting eugenics but I don't know where they're going now. There's talk of a rogue faction, a group calling themselves 'Les Rouges'. Skanky scuttlebutt says they got to 'rouge' by misspelling 'rogue'.

JOSEPHINE: Maybe they're dyslexic too? But ... in any case, Lobak did suck up all the air time.

ANTHONY: I wonder if it was a purposeful diversion? All that attention forced onto you. It meant less attention to eugenics. And to technological progress.

JOSEPHINE: Your ideas about technological improvement are a devil's mish-mash of racism and narcissism. You haven't addressed the complexity.

ANTHONY: What about the freedom for research that the deformed and the diseased — themselves! — want carried out?

JOSEPHINE: Progress isn't always about technology. The social fabric, conviviality, counts. Did you not notice that whenever one sector tyrannizes, the other gnaws back?

Gertrude takes them to Chicago. They decide to ride the El to get an overview of the city. When the train goes under the Chicago River, they zip past a sequence of drawings zoetropically animated. A stick figure rolls along in a wheelchair, then vigorously stands up, and finally runs away from the wheelchair. Followed by dancing renderings, in pastel and paisley, of the words: 'The Step Beyond!' and 'OR ELSE!'

A video of the zoetrope goes viral. The Nightly News reports it as an artistic novelty and a clever graffiti hack by the unknown group, Les Rouges. Following the news, the pundits pontificate.

SAGACIOUS PUNDIT: That 'Or Else' sounds ominous. Who are these people?

PUGILISTIC PUNDIT: Little is known about 'Les Rouges'. Maybe a play on words, scientists gone rogue.

SAGACIOUS PUNDIT: Maybe they are just rogue graffiti vandals. More important, the matter at hand is about the hacking, so to speak, at the Citizen House. It looks like poor little Ms. Josephine got set up.

PUGILISTIC PUNDIT: That goes to show that the Citizen House needs more representatives. The Athenians… They are shibboleths, like our Founding Fathers… The Athenians didn't need the Assembly to be as large as it was. They could get up to 20% of their population into the Pynx where they voted. 6,000 of the 30,000 citizens.

PUGILISTIC PUNDIT: Why did they need such a large percentage to vote?

SAGACIOUS PUNDIT: Because it's difficult to bribe that many people. That's why. But remember that proposals – what we call 'bills' -- were formulated by only 500. And they were sortitionally chosen. That's less than two percent.

PUGILISTIC PUNDIT: Our Citizen House is also composed of 500. But with our population, representation is an infinitesimal percentage of the entire population. One rep for every 700,000-plus.

SAGACIOUS PUNDIT: If we followed the Athenian example of their Assembly, we would have a legislature of sixty-four million! Twenty percent.

STATELY PUNDIT: And even if we emulated the policy-making body of the Athenians, only 2% of the population, we'd still have a group of over five million.

PUGILISTIC PUNDIT: In other words, the Athenians prevented bribery by ensuring mass participation. Personal trustworthiness was beside the point in that situation.

SAGACIOUS PUNDIT: Yeah, yeah, yeah. OK, you're right.

PUGILISTIC PUNDIT: But we've only got the 500. A well-funded, determined small group of lobbyists can have an out-sized influence. Or, if you're an NGO, you can call them 'advocates'. Josephine is a case in point.

SAGACIOUS PUNDIT: Doesn't matter that she was found innocent. The damage has been done.

STATELY PUNDIT: And then there is crazy talk about a military coup. Anything to bring attention to the opposition.

From under the table, he pulls out a small fish. Painted red.

STATELY PUNDIT: It's a herring.

He swallows it.

STATELY PUNDIT: Food coloring.

And laughs.

Josephine and Anthony on Gertrude, past midnight. They are playing cards.

JOSEPHINE: I think what we have to do is to create a phase-locked loop.

ANTHONY: A what?

JOSEPHINE: A phase-locked loop.

ANTHONY: Get serious, woman. We don't have much time left.

JOSEPHINE: What it is… is … you can keep things in order, even if everything you have is inaccurate and unreliable. It's called phase lock looping. It works with clocks and it looks like it is working – unbeknownst and unasked – between the two of us.

At Lobak's Washington headquarters.

LOBAK #1: Since the Citizen House isn't going to vote itself out of existence, we're going to have to have set up a constitutional convention.

LOBAK #2: No, you're wrong. That would be hard. What we ought to do is set up a national referendum.

LOBAK #1: The Constitution doesn't admit of a national referendum.

LOBAK #2: Not so. The Constitution begins with 'We, the People.' Article Five does not limit a direct national vote. The argument for a direct decree by The People is constitutionally sound. Article Five presupposes that The People are sovereign.

LOBAK #1: Who's going to sanction its credibility?

LOBAK #2: Sure, questions will arise, but we think the courts will allow it. Don't forget that the executive is stronger than this hodgepodge legislature. The Department of Justice can be persuaded not to mount much of a defense. You think we could still use the Election Commission to assure credibility?

She laughs.

LOBAK #1: Yeah, I guess so.

LOBAK #2 So it is, after all, a governmentally sanctioned election… instituting a federal level referendum. A.k.a., a direct decree.

The President has lunch at the Pentagon with the Joint Chiefs.

JOINT CHIEF: Why do they always, The People, seem to look upon us as either their saviors or their overlords?

THE PRESIDENT: The people tend to forget that the military is controlled by civilians. In a democracy.

60

JOINT CHIEF: Which is why we find ourselves now in the predicament of a leaderless legislature, adrift in petty debates about a million different ideas. I think, gentlemen, it may be time for more vigorous action on our parts.

The Joint Chiefs give a 'hear, hear!'

In Anacostia, in their ordinary home, as they lay in bed on their way to sleep, a man tells his wife what he heard in his role as the Waiter who served the President and the Joint Chiefs during that lunch.

WAITER'S WIFE: Maybe you should alert one of the Citizen House legislators?

WAITER: Who am I going to tell? The rep who is most 'like me' comes from Massachusetts. But she's gone home with the rest of them. Besides, I don't want to lose my job. That confidentiality clause in my contract...

In the next room, three young children sleep soundly.

WAITER: I love you, honey. Good night.

Their bedside clock reads midnight.

Josephine and Anthony are still playing cards on Gertrude.

ANTHONY: OK, I bite. Tell me more.

JOSEPHINE: Let's say you've got an inaccurate timer, like a pendulum. With a small amount of added mechanical energy it will continue indefinitely. But without occasional adjustment it will drift.

Josephine is into it.

JOSEPHINE: All you need, however, to assure the correct time over very long time periods is a timer which may be unreliable but is accurate. Like solar alignment. High noon is absolutely accurate. Always. If you lock those two in phase with each other, you'll get perfection.

ANTHONY: What do you mean, 'lock in phase'.

JOSEPHINE: High noon is unreliable because of the possibility of cloud cover. Or even years-long dust clouds... maybe caused by volcanic eruption, large meteor impact or, God forbid, nuclear winter. But eventually that daily high noon will reappear. It will then adjust an inaccurate but reliable one -- a pendulum driven by a bimetallic lever powered by diurnal temperature differences.

ANTHONY: Brilliant!

Lobak at their DC headquarters.
LOBAK #1: There will always be some who have more than others. We are providing the template for all the world to follow. Leading the pack, we are morally and duty-bound. Some have to. The Elect.

LOBAK #2: Many see us as rescuers of the republic.
Lobak media issues ads celebrating the country's military and supposed economic dominance. And promoting a return to elections for the lower chamber.

One ad features testimonials from purported everyday people, each one portrayed in their identifying environment.
TRAILER COURT RESIDENT: Thing about election campaigns… Even if it's a nasty, hostile campaign… there is a good deal of information delivered. You learn stuff about the government. Elections force the politicians to come to The People. They've got to educate everyone.

FORMER POLITICIAN: Without the competition — and the energy generated — of elections, do you think ordinary citizens would pay any attention to the boring, dull business of day-to-day legislating? No, most people would pay attention to their own tasks. They would leave legislation up to the legislators. It's only when things get a little heated up, like now, when people hit the streets.

GAS STATION OWNER: With sortition, what you get is the average. 'Average', as in 'mediocre'. In all ways: intelligence, income, identity and so on. But let me tell you that America was set up based on hard-work and get-ahead. On meritocracy, on struggle for the top. Not on reaching those guys in the middle.

SCHOOL TEACHER: America was always meant to be great, to be the gold standard of what human existence is all about, what it is tending towards. America is the cutting edge of human evolution!

In a sports bar, a young man is thrown off a mechanical bull. The aforementioned ad is concluding.
YOUNG MAN: God, I'm tired of hearing that sort of claptrap. As if all the 99% of The People who emigrated from the

east — and pushed out the 1% of indigenous who hadn't been wiped out by disease or outright genocide — as if all of us more recently arrived… are somehow transformed into humans better than all those relatives who didn't quite make it across the ocean, or the Bering Strait before it turned water again.

YOUNG WOMAN: Thomas Paine promoted civil society. He saw government as the problem.

YOUNG MAN: Paine was limited by his individualistic liberalism. He didn't realize that government power could serve less abusive ends.

YOUNG WOMAN: Rousseau linked 'the general will' with a benign government.

YOUNG MAN: Precisely. A statistically representative legislature is that perfect expression of the general will. The government is The People.

YOUNG WOMAN: Paine failed to see the possibility of nongovernmental threats to freedom, equality, and democracy.

YOUNG MAN: Paine's limitation, if you want to call it that, was that he was passionately and radically opposed to privilege of all sorts.

YOUNG WOMAN: Well, that being the case… regarding instituting eugenic improvements… he would have been against it since only rich folk could afford it.

YOUNG MAN: He would have required the government to subsidize the technologic cost of genetic enhancement to ensure its equitable availability.

YOUNG WOMAN: Yes, he would.

In the National Parks, remnants of the protesting occupation drag on. Pitifully. They've trashed all they've touched.

PROTESTER: Too many are dopers.

The tattered signs droop. It's a mess. Only a few stragglers hold on.

The same at the Pentagon. A bedraggled tent city.

The National Guard takes over.

The Corps of Engineers dismantles everything.

Josephine folds up her cards. Anthony takes a final sip of tea.

JOSEPHINE: So… OK. You, Anthony, are that unreliable but accurate actor. Emotionally damaged, but educationally rich. You and I have, despite our differences, locked up, in phase, into a loop with each other. I am the inaccurate but reliable actor. Emotionally healthy but educationally lacking.
She flips the joker from the deck of cards at him.

JOSEPHINE: Bingo! It may have taken us a while. But we can reconcile!

ANTHONY: That easy, hey?

At their DC headquarters Lobak #1, #2 and #3 hold a video conference call. The calendar shows early August.

LOBAK #1: Only two weeks until they're scheduled to re-convene. We've got to strike now. All out. The protesters are waning. Any blowback, push-back, backfire… has got to happen now. Otherwise we'll be punching a ball of cotton candy.

LOBAK #2: Right. The direct decree looks good, it's taking off. But it's not assured. We need to keep the fright level up.

LOBAK #1: If we could get the President to declare something like a state of emergency. Or dismiss the legislature. That would do it.

LOBAK #2: It can't be done. We aren't a parliamentary system.

LOBAK #3: Right, we aren't. But there is a way. Article Two, Section Three. The President can call a special session of one or both houses. If the two Houses cannot agree on a date for adjournment, the President may adjourn either or both Houses to such a time as befits the circumstances.

LOBAK #1: Ah! So we'll make sure our friends in the Senate cannot agree with the House. The President then adjourns the House. And the Senate declares a state of emergency.

LOBAK #3: Then the national guard enacts martial law. Based on the traitorous activity of these people led by Josephine and by Anthony.

LOBAK #1: In the meantime, we keep the ideological pressure on. Have you seen what we arranged for our science guy out in the Midwest?

Anthony and Josephine return to Washington.
ANTHONY: My friends have used me. They want to take everything.
JOSEPHINE: Oh?
ANTHONY: I just wanted us, everyone… to progress.
They descend into blackest gloom.
JOSEPHINE and ANTHONY (simultaneously): Common ground?
JOSEPHINE: Sure, yes, ha-ha. You the Person of Color…
ANTHONY: In a wheelchair.
JOSEPHINE: And me, the Person of No Color…
ANTHONY: With dyslexia.
JOSEPHINE: Well, why not?
ANTHONY: Common ground?

Newspapers and television and social media are full of stories denouncing Josephine and Anthony and the Citizen House. Lobak-controlled media attack most viciously.
There are nonetheless also many remaining adherents who remain suspicious of Lobak. Especially on social media. These suspicions are heightened by rumors about a rogue faction of Lobak that is calling for more vigorous action regarding eugenics. Social media has millions of hits of the 'The Step Beyond' zoetrope on the subway line.
According to internet postings, Les Rouges claims to represent a spontaneous order, more authentic, more grounded, more emergent … than the main Lobak faction. The messages include a threat of 'dire consequences' if 'free independent research for the betterment of all mankind' is not allowed.
Les Rouges establishes its own website with a communiqué and a video interview.
ONLINE LES ROUGES COMMUNIQUE: We believe in an advanced vision. The Step Beyond. Not only is it a human right that every child has the right to be born free of preventable diseases. We

go beyond that. Towards artificial intelligence, singularity, immortality!

A 'click here' brings up a video interview with all faces covered by bandanas.

LES ROUGES JOYEUX: There are of course the simple gene therapy techniques that the main faction of Lobak wants unregulated. But what Les Rouges wants is germ-line gene engineering.

LES ROUGES INDISCIPLINE: We are talking about not just curing individuals of HIV, genetic blindness, sickle-cell anemia and hemophilia. No. We are talking about enhancing the human race. The curing of individuals are mere 'edits'.

LES ROUGES ENTHOUSIASTE: Others have said it before. We need to follow the example of the more adventurous. In other countries they already do embryo editing. Affecting evolution itself. That could permanently eliminate genetic maladies like Huntington's disease and cystic fibrosis.

LES ROUGES JOYEUX: These devastating genetically-caused illnesses can be permanently defeated.

LES ROUGES ENTHOUSIASTE: But beyond that, we believe in developing self-replicating nanotechnology, robots.

NAY-SAYER STOOGE: And how will you avoid unleashing ecophagic nano-robots? That is to say, robots that consume everything. Libertarians may oppose constraints on research. But how do we deal with the logical extension of 'curiosity killed the cat'.

LES ROUGES ENTHOUSIASTE: What, you got a problem with cats?

NAY-SAYER STOOGE: No, actually I love watching cat videos. Check this out.

He puts on a video of a cat approaching a downed electrical wire, sniffing, poking and ... electrocuting itself.

LES ROUGES ENTHOUSIASTE: Ha. Ha. Sick!

LES ROUGES JOYEUX: So are you saying that science will kill itself?

ANOTHER NAY-SAYER STOOGE: Let's just say that for nanotech to fully develop, the government must be involved as a major player. At this stage, only they can make molecular assemblers.

ANOTHER NAY-SAYER STOOGE: But once they are made… then anybody can make the universal assemblers. Result… End of the world. Grey goop.

LES ROUGES JOYEUX: Show me, I'm from Missouri.

NAY-SAYER STOOGE: Unh. Only in theory.

Nay-sayer plays another video, full of post-production weirdness. The ecophagic result: Grey Goop.

LES ROUGES JOYEUX: Germ-line genetic engineering requires closed doors. They have to rejigger genes.

LES ROUGES INDISCIPLINE: Democracy depends on free actors.

NAY-SAYER STOOGE: Democracy is less important than existence, wouldn't you say?

ANOTHER NAY-SAYER STOOGE: At this point the question for an engineered human being becomes: 'WHO are you? Really?'

LES ROUGES JOYEUX: Oh, 'really'? How is that now? Just how much control did you have over the parental DNA that mingled to create you? How is that different from those parents making a decision to insert, to splice, something else into you?

NAY-SAYER STOOGE: Well, you'd never know, would you?

ANOTHER NAY-SAYER STOOGE: And would that matter?

LES ROUGES ENTHOUSIASTE: But does the universe care?

NAY-SAYER STOOGE: What is the universe?

LES ROUGES INDISCIPLINE: Transhumanism leads to the post-human. It's evolution on steroids, directed by humans.

LES ROUGES ENTHOUSIASTE: Artificial intelligence with the ability to improve upon its own design will rapidly lead to super-intelligence. Reaching this 'singularity' is the best way to minimize net existential risk. In other words, eugenics meshes with AI for the long term goal of transcendence!

LES ROUGES JOYEUX: Nothing dogmatic here, nothing religious. Just what it is.

NAY-SAYER STOOGE: Don't give me that. You're full on into the religious. It's rapture for the techies! You guys, you libertarians…

LES ROUGES INDISCIPLINE: A civil right to enhancement.

LES ROUGES ENTHOUSIASTE: The free market is the best guarantor.

LES ROUGES INDISCIPLINE: You might say we believe in self-ownership. Nobody can steal us, our essence, but ourselves. Do you object to that?

NAY-SAYER STOOGE: You might say so. Yeah. That. And your selfishness. Your elitism. Your escapism.

ANOTHER NAY-SAYER STOOGE: Transhumanists advocate merciless meritocracy. They despair of finding social and political solutions. Everything is reduced to an hereditary dream. It's a fantasy of omnipotence.

And thus the night wears on.

At the headquarters of Lobak, Anthony witnesses the widening split between the original leaders and Les Rouges. The mainstream of Lobak posts a two-pronged warning on its website. The text is blunt. But the subtext is subtle. A photograph of the U.S. Navy's steamship of 1864-65, Isonomia, heads the site. It seems that Lobak supports the rule of law as well as the law of nature.

LOBAK WEBSITE: Beware the blind worship of progress. A nuanced approach to the pursuit of knowledge avoids turning science into an idol. Beware those who want not only to subdue Nature, but to exceed it.

Anthony telephones Josephine.

ANTHONY: Things are out of control. Democracy is in danger. What if the President dissolves the Congress?

JOSEPHINE: He can't. The closest thing he might do is suspend legal protections against being held. Article 1.9… 'The Privilege of the Writ of Habeas Corpus shall not be suspended, unless when in Cases of Rebellion or Invasion the public Safety may require it.' But he can't shut down Congress. A ruling by the

Supreme Court, just after Civil War, established that only Congress can suspend habeas corpus. Lincoln had done so five years earlier, in the war.

ANTHONY: Yes, but Article 1, Section 3 says if, when the President convenes both houses, and the two houses can not agree on an adjournment date, then the President can adjourn either house. She could adjourn only the Citizen House, leaving the Senate to call for suspension of habeas corpus.

ANTHONY: Would that then be effectively martial law?

JOSEPHINE: Indeed.

Anthony snarls.

ANTHONY: Lovely.

After they hang up, Anthony and Josephine separately despair, each bereft and alone, in confrontation with a moral abyss.

All around the nation, workers are setting up polling stations for the direct decree. In Washington, Lobak #1 looks out the window of headquarters. Gardeners are working the lawn.

LOBAK #1: With our friends in the state houses, it's no problem to get the moronic electorate to repeal the amendment.

LOBAK #2: The expense is taken care of. Our multinational donors are footing the bill. The same ones whose lawyers helped us draft the repeal.

LOBAK #3: Of course we can't succeed in the normal way, with little nudges to convince Congressmen to vote one way or the other. The Citizen House is in recess and they wouldn't, anyway, vote for their own suicide.

LOBAK #1: The state legislatures have soured, now that they see what they've lost. They see clearly now. What they created. This monstrosity of a non-elected House.

In an undisclosed location in the basement of a funeral home that is re-decorated as a faux beer hall, a couple dozen members of Les Rouges are yucking it up, bleating out a round of 'Roll Out The Barrel'.

Les Rouges Joyeux holds up her hands, laughing, interrupting. Holding them in suspension, she inserts a DVD into the entertainment console. 'Fantasia' -- the animation of 1940 –

appears without sound on the wall screen. Mickey Mouse is the cockamamie wizard, replicating broom sticks in a rising flood. Les Rouge breaks into a different song.

LES ROUGES: Hi Ho, Hi Ho, it's off to work we go!

LES ROUGES JOYEUX: They think they're in a pickle now. Just wait. Their pickle is going to turn to putsch!

LES ROUGES ENTHOUSIASTE: How many sides are there in the current political arrangement?

LES ROUGES JOYEUX: The military, for one. Even though somewhat divided our claim to meritocratic legitimacy keeps most of them loyal.

LES ROUGES INDISIPLINE: Ho, Ho! Jolly Jo!

LES ROUGES ENTHOUSIASTE: Then there's the Eugenicists. Sweet people, all the best interests for the best of the human race.

LES ROUGES JOYEUX: And the Fabulists, a.k.a. the Egalitarians.

He spits.

LES ROUGES INDISCIPLINE: The Libertarians, in the Eugenicist camp. Who else?

LES ROUGES JOYEUX: You forgot the Academics!

LES ROUGES ENTHOUSIASTE: And the Peripatetics. Gotta have the Peripatetics.

LES ROUGES JOYEUX: The Epicureans. A taste of honey, know what I mean?

LES ROUGES INDISCIPLINE: The Stoics. Straighten up!

LES ROUGES ENTHOUSIASTE: Logicians!

LES ROUGES INDISCIPLINE: Strategists!

LES ROUGES JOYEUX: The whole point is we get protection for the laboratory. The singularity, coming right up!

LES ROUGES ENTHOUSIASTE: The Step Beyond!

LES ROUGES INDISCIPLINE: With Josephine as house guest!

They collapse in merriment.

In Washington a headline scrolls on the marquee of the Newseum: 'Based on 'revolutionary threat' gone underground, president calls Congress back to special session.'

A day later, the headline scrolls: 'Senate and House can not agree on date of adjournment.'

A day later, the headline scrolls: 'President uses power to adjourn Citizen House.' And: 'Senate begins debate on possible suspension of habeas corpus.'

Les Rouges issues a communiqué.
LES ROUGES COMMUNIQUE: War is the health of the State. Capitalism demands expansion. Our libertarian forefathers declared that we can not crusade against war without implicitly crusading against the State. Our anti-war position represents a truly pro-American stance on foreign policy.

SEPTEMBER

Josephine answers an invitation to a surprise birthday party at the home of a congressional colleague. When she has to use the bathroom, Les Rouges lock her in. Then they put her in a dog cage. It is the implementation of their Operation Jolly Jo.

The Senate goes rhetorically ballistic. The taking of a member of the legislature as hostage exposes personal apprehensions. The debate on suspension of habeas corpus summarily concludes. Habeas corpus is dead.

The police swoop in, making arrests upon citizens and journalists on suspicion of aiding the kidnapping.

Josephine sits in the dog cage in the Indianapolis laboratory of Les Rouges.
LES ROUGES JOYEUX: We thought that would be a nice touch, the cage.
LES ROUGES INDISCIPLINE: Crate. The media likes 'crate'. More humane than 'cage'.
LES ROUGES JOYEUX: Right.
Josephine doesn't take it sitting down. She yells.

71

JOSEPHINE: You think you can take me hostage? Hell, I've been a hostage my whole life. But guess what? I'm breaking the law. I'm a thief, stealing myself. No matter what you do, you can't touch me.

LES ROUGES JOYEUX: Oh, yeah? How you gonna do that, sister?

JOSEPHINE: Don't 'sister' me!

Anthony creeps, guardedly, into Lobak headquarters. With none of the Lobak members daring to stand close to him, he nonetheless holds his ground. All eyes are glued on a large monitor suspended behind a well-stocked liquor bar.
On the screen, robed men and women of grave demeanor sit in line behind a long wooden dais. Superimposed on the video image: 'The People's Tribunal'. It's a make-shift courtroom scene, rigged by Les Rouges. With Josephine in the dock.

When the kangaroo court is over, Lobak holds a press conference. They abjure relations with their former colleagues in Les Rouges and they decry the hostage-taking. They say they want to proceed more carefully.

As soon as the press conference ends, these Lobak leaders are arrested by deputized members of the National Guard. They are jailed without benefit of habeas corpus.

Anthony's interest in eugenics has taken a back seat now since he has come to realize his social standing has protected him from the difficulties that Josephine has endured.

LOBAK #1: Hitler dismissed the entry of the United States into the war. Because, he said, we were – and still are -- a country of mongrels.

ANTHONY: Oh, really?

Lobak #1 grins devilishly.

LOBAK #1: Oh, not you, Tony. Not you. Not me.

Lobak #1 can hardly restrain his disdain for Anthony.

ANTHONY: Hitler meant that hybridization of the races — miscegenation, to be precise — would dilute, not strengthen. Thing is, genetic engineering is hybridization, exponentially.

Anthony holds a press conference on the sidewalk outside LOBAK headquarters.

ANTHONY: There is always the need for societal agreement about these things. Mutually-agreed rules. That is called making laws. I plead with all rational people: regulated eugenics will bring peace and prosperity to all.

A member of Lobak interrupts Anthony.

LOBAK #2: Libertarians aren't known for cozying up to the regulators. Are you sure you want to say what you said?

ANTHONY: Well, if ever there were some reason … it might be for saving lives. For people alive now. You may know that it won't be long before the technology becomes so accessible that you'll see a bioterrorist strap a biologic bomb to himself. One that, if activated, could run havoc, killing hundreds of millions, maybe billions, maybe every living thing. Tell me there shouldn't be some restraint, some 'regulation' if you will, to protect against that?

On a cable television news and opinion show, standing next to elaborate animated graphics to which they make frequent hyperventilating reference, a male and a female pundit give an overview of the political situation.

FEMALE PUNDIT: Josephine sits as a prisoner. What happens next is complicated. It's called a Prisoner's Dilemma. To understand it we have to tell you about Game Studies.

MALE PUNDIT: It's not just a matter of two imprisoned accomplices, incommunicado with each other. Not a one time run-through of 'Did you or didn't you?' No, it's iterated. One question and consequent answer leads to another.

FEMALE PUNDIT: It requires repeated inquiry among multiple players. It turns out that greedy strategies fail in the long run. And altruistic strategies succeed.

MALE PUNDIT: But if it's just one-on-one, then retribution succeeds. But that's not what we've got in a complex society such as ours. What we've got here, with Joseph and Anthony, is an inter-temporal Prisoner's Dilemma between the present and future.

FEMALE PUNDIT: This is important politically since it dovetails with the dominant economic paradigms. Either social control via government interference. Or social control via spontaneous order. The latter also known as the free market or, philosophically, as Emergence. Both paradigms include the rules of play.

MALE PUNDIT: This scenario between Anthony and Josephine is complicated by the interpersonal relationship that has grown between them. Prisoner's Dilemma generally does not go beyond rational choices.

FEMALE PUNDIT: The key to understanding this is knowing what it means to 'Stay true' or 'To defect'. 'Staying true' means, for Anthony, not coming to Josephine's aid. We don't know what her fate is. 'Staying true' for Anthony means going along with it, sticking with his faction, becoming a Top Dog in the actual political system and accomplishing his goal of unfettered development of eugenics. In that way he maintains his self-esteem.

MALE PUNDIT: 'Staying true' for Josephine means staying in captivity but doing something to save herself and, at the same time possibly leading to re-establishing the Citizen House and eventually her drive for income equality. It's a big lift but in this way she would maintain her self-esteem.

FEMALE PUNDIT: 'Defecting' for Anthony means abandoning his faction and rushing to Josephine's aid. Which means also giving up the freedom to pursue eugenics. In this scenario the Citizen House is perhaps re-established but it would nonetheless be deeply constrained by his moneyed cohort. He loses self-esteem for disloyalty. Something like defecating.

MALE PUNDIT: Ew!

FEMALE PUNDIT: Sorry. I meant 'defecting'.

MALE PUNDIT: OK, yeah. Anyway… 'Defecting' for Josephine means staying silent for the sake of going-along-to-get-along and thereby accomplishing her own release. Perhaps a truncated or eviscerated Citizen House would be re-established. But she loses her self-esteem for disloyalty.

Female Pundit points to a graphic.

FEMALE PUNDIT: So those are the four axials.

MALE PUNDIT: But then we've got to add in the effect of the systemic bias that afflicts all humans. Anthony is torn between maintaining his overly high self-esteem — that is, what he thought of himself, as a humanist libertarian — and his recognition that Josephine has the same goal and equally high self-esteem.

FEMALE PUNDIT: To say nothing, or rather to say something, about the opposition's dilemma.

She gives a wink-wink and blatantly mouths 'LOBAK'.

FEMALE PUNDIT: For them 'staying true' means stability of hierarchy, even with its attendant high cost. 'Defecting' means a return to democratic messiness but with an ability to manipulate.

MALE PUNDIT: To wrap it up, this is what got us here. The Citizen House was established. Ran into the sticky wicket about accountability. The People split into apathetics and activists. Some sought repeal of the sortitionist amendment. Then Josephine was kidnapped. With Les Rouges demanding a Free State. Whatever that is.

FEMALE PUNDIT: Right, whatever that is…

MALE PUNDIT: We need to remember that Josephine and Anthony are ordinary people. Not politicians who earned their way by winning an election.

FEMALE PUNDIT: Does this mean that their ordinariness should be implicated in… however-it-is that they manage to overcome the threat?

MALE PUNDIT: A correction. True, without sortition people like Josephine would not be in the legislature. But people like Anthony would!

FEMALE PUNDIT: Good point. The deliberative model does tend to reinforce the power of the socially-advantaged. Education, rhetorical ability, class distinctions… none of that goes away when randomly selected groups gather.

MALE PUNDIT: Even, in the first place, the option to place in the pool for random selection… that skews it. Even merely the good-looking will tend to dominate discussions.

FEMALE PUNDIT: Yes, exactly. Josephine and Anthony have to answer to different inquisitors.

MALE PUNDIT: And we haven't specified that the interest groups, formerly held together in political parties, also still hold sway.

FEMALE PUNDIT: It's not that those five hundred representatives all have views on the disparate questions that come before them. They follow advice of advocacy groups. Or merely the proclivities of friend and acquaintances.

MALE PUNDIT: Same old horse trading as the old bunch.

FEMALE PUNDIT: Lobbyists, advocates, civil society, non-profits...

MALE PUNDIT: And so on.

FEMALE PUNDIT: To vote one way or the other, for instance, on libertarian eugenics, the focused advocates are for de-regulation to the max.

MALE PUNDIT: And for Universal Basic Income, regulation to the max.

FEMALE PUNDIT: LOBAK is inadvertently forcing them into a united front!

MALE PUNDIT: Josephine and Anthony are even talking about 'doing common ground' together!

His compatriot shouts.

FEMALE PUNDIT: Lordy! Lordy! It must be the millennium coming.

MALE PUNDIT: Good thing, since we seem to have missed the last one.

In their Indianapolis redoubt, Les Rouges continue issuing demands for guaranteed protection of their lab. One of them explain their actions on Facebook.

LES ROUGES JOYEUX: As a traitor to the cause of human betterment, we hold representative Josephine under house arrest.

At their lab, Les Rouges complete an elaborate system of booby traps and emplaced weaponry. They issue a video of a 'biological bomb' that could unleash an omnicidal bacterium.

The media both tut-tuts and blames Jo for her captivity.

NEWCASTER ONE: She asked for it. She went along with the tax refusal movement. She's a legislator -- charged with assuring the government's income and supposedly a guardian of the Rule of Law. How irresponsible!

NEWCASTER TWO: The Universal Basic Income shows itself all the more to be nothing but a free ride for the freeloaders. Its proponents are nothing more than ne'er-do-wells, these so-called

76

libertarian 'mountain men' and the natives seeking restitution… all those that have been unleashed by Anthony's gambit.

This reporting continues to undermine public support to free 'Jolly Jo'.

Nonetheless, more supporters of Les Rouges are placed in jail, without right of habeas corpus.

Inside the constrained circumstances of her captivity, Josephine befriends the Young Daughter of one member of Les Rouges. The girl's asymmetric face and out-of-kilter skull are the result of Thalessimia, a genetically-inherited disorder. She diddles on a computer tablet.

JOSEPHINE: You like school?

YOUNG DAUGHTER: I like video games.

JOSEPHINE: You play on the internet?

YOUNG DAUGHTER: I always win.

JOSEPHINE: Will you help me send a message on your computer?

At that moment, the Joyeux member of Les Rouge suddenly enters the room.

LES ROUGES JOYEUX: Go right ahead. My daughter could use a little companionship. No one else will give it to her.

Joyeux hands Josephine a pen and paper.

Josephine writes: 'All in, bingo vel. Rongse are treatiug usOK. We ~~uebe~~… I call for nouvioleut occuqaiton of Rongse ladortoray.'

Joyeux looks at the dyslexic message. She picks up her daughter's tablet, enters an email address and hands it back to her daughter.

LES ROUGES JOYEUX: Sure, send out that mess.

Young Daughter quietly enters Jo's message into her device.

LES ROUGES JOYEUX: How did you ever make it as a waitress?

Josephine bristles.

JOSEPHINE: Some of us know honest work.

Joyeux snorts a laugh.

LES ROUGES JOYEUX: Trailer trash.

Young Daughter hits 'send'.

Off it goes.

Anthony sits in his Washington apartment in front of a soundless television news program. But his eyes are on the computer in his lap. Suddenly he laughs, the same kind of laugh Les Rouges Joyeux had just laughed, hundreds of miles away.

Anthony opens a search engine and types 'Auto correct for dyslexia'. He looks up at the TV, is startled. He interrupts the computer search and gives a voice command.

ANTHONY: Un-mute.

TV NEWS REPORTER: According to medical research released today, muscle degeneration in several debilitating diseases is caused by maladaptive genetic recombination.

A complicated graphic appears on the screen.

TV NEWS REPORTER: This is an outline of the technique used, called somatic cell manipulation. The muscle degeneration can be halted by conventional gene therapy that uses active cells and is not inheritable.

Another complicated graphic appears.

TV NEWS REPORTER: This shows an additional medical intervention called germline-gene therapy. This therapy can prevent the inheritance of the disease. The report warns, however, that this additional treatment has unknown long-term evolutionary consequences.

Anthony mutes the TV, goes to his bedroom closet, pulls out a large box and begins rifling through memorabilia. He finds the scorched baseball mitt.
He cries.

The betrayal by his parents has discolored his entire life. His eugenicist friends have only played upon that betrayal. He grieves for having debased himself in misusing Josephine.

In his automobile, equipped to drive without use of his legs, he drives himself to the state park where, so long ago, his mother accidentally set the wildfire. He wheels himself on a long trail, paved for the disabled, into the forest.

The tree canopy filters the sunlight into a green haze. He stops to listen to a birdsong. His eyes open wide, bedazzled by the conjunction. Birdsong. Forest light. The park where his mother had betrayed him.

He envisions that fire. The end of it. Embers fading. The wildfire of his childhood. The fire that enflamed a ridiculous, superior, human, being.

He breaks. Solitary. Sobbing.

When he returns from the park, he finds a reporter at his door. Before the reporter has a chance to ask a question, Anthony launches forth

ANTHONY: I mean we only want happiness and freedom. I thought that was the whole purpose behind Lobak. Guess I was wrong. I recall a film about a donkey. When I was a kid. Black-and-white. French. At the end, the donkey dies.

The memory halts him. He stutters.

ANTHONY: I have come… eugenics only creates… physical change. We need a moral change. Unalloyed pragmatism doesn't… No sparks of the unknown.

The polling stations are set to open in a few days. Pundits pretend to know what will happen. But their predictions cancel each other.

Anthony releases Josephine's message calling for citizens to nonviolently occupy the laboratory of Les Rogues and thereby end her kidnapped confinement. He posts her message on his website.

JOSEPHINE'S MESSAGE: This may be the first time that dyslexia has been the means of issuing a revolutionary message. I suppose it is not exactly one of the Great Ironies of History. But… what the hey? Compared to the Dred Scott decision — making it illegal to steal oneself — it'll do.

People respond to her call. A huge nonviolent siege of laboratory. People of all ideological stripes, religious and otherwise. Some are laying on cots, fasting.
Les Rouges continues issuing threats. They say the laboratory is mined, ready to explode if breached. The authorities withhold frontal assault.

Anthony joins in the nonviolent siege of the laboratory. He becomes the leader. The People refer to him as 'Ant'. Industrious and reliable.
The occupiers wait out the hostage takers.
Days go by.
A uniformed policeman walks towards the compound. A shot rings out. He goes down, clutching his leg, suddenly bleeding profusely.
'Ant' demonstrates his commitment by willing to sacrifice himself to rescue Josephine. 'Ant' rolls himself into the line of fire. Les Rouges taser him. He falls out of his wheelchair, convulsing on the floor. Everyone is immobilized, in shock.
From out of the crowd, then the little girl with the deformed skull appears. Slowly she walks towards the Les Rouges shooter. She gets closer and closer as the shooter points his taser at her.
He cannot fire.
She disarms him.
The crowd pours in and dismantles the laboratory.
The little girl reaches to the policeman, gets her hand bloody, wipes her mouth, tastes it. Shocked, she stares.
The policeman stands right up, no longer in any pain, no longer faking it, the reality of a 'Tokugawa fusillade'. He runs away, his role of accomplice to Les Rouges exposed.

The polls open. Voters vote. The polls close.
The direct decree to repeal the sortition amendment is defeated by a landslide.

Habeas corpus is reinstated. The formerly arrested stream out of jails. Signs and placards for various and conflicting causes proliferate.

Josephine and Anthony share a meal at a restaurant in Washington.
JOSEPHINE: Well, that wasn't so bad, was it?
ANTHONY: No, it wasn't. My erstwhile buddies in Lobak have gone back to their palatial sewers.

80

JOSEPHINE: Our colleagues in The Citizen House will need to keep an eye on them. I think we can expect that they will be in their haunts, licking their wounds, for a long time to come.

ANTHONY: True.

JOSEPHINE: Do you think they will suffer any retribution from the masses?

ANTHONY: No, I don't think so. The 99% are not retributive. The Citizen House is just another step along the progression from universal suffrage to universal deliberation. Once the 'mass' -- lately of 'the masses' -- comes to grips with it, gets good at it, becomes 'One'... Oh, boy, then we're going to see true 'singularity'. Humanity as one coherent organism aware of its own self-worth and willing to sacrifice for the sake of all beings, sentient and otherwise. It's worth noting that 'one coherent organism' emerges organically as a result of heterogeneity. That is, through conflict and disruption. Peacefulness, in other words, in not the goal. Stasis is death.

JOSEPHINE: Awf!

Anthony smiles.

NOVEMBER

A cold wind blows as Anthony and Josephine brave a walk along the Washington DC waterfront. She carries a plastic bag.

ANTHONY: If I ever decide to have children, I will adopt. I've decided against accepting germ-line gene therapy. It comes down to evolutionary biology. You've got emergence...

JOSEPHINE: You mean internally driven gene fluctuation.

ANTHONY: Right. And you've got natural selection. That's about meeting basic needs. My focus has been on the former. About messing with genes.

JOSEPHINE: And mine has been on the latter. About providing basic livelihood.

ANTHONY: Genetic diversity, even with its downsides, is required. It's not merely 'dearly wished' or 'a nice touch' or even 'justified'.

JOSEPHINE: Nature hates a monoculture. Human humility is a necessity for survival. As banal as it is to say it, we will never ever know everything.

They approach a barrel fire maintained by the homeless under a freeway. Josephine opens her plastic bag and tosses her high heel shoes into the fire.

JOSEPHINE: Won't need those anymore. Road trip is over.

ANTHONY: I've pulled out my old baseball mitt. A little scorched but useable. I'm going to join a wheelchair softball league.

JOSEPHINE: I was a waitress. I am still a waitress. I thought those shoes were a sign of my liberation, no longer had to wear flats all day. Could once in a while get out to a club, click my heels, high heels. Could be one of them, could be served.

ANTHONY: We can forgive but we will not forget. That is the requirement for a successful civil society. All in.

JOSEPHINE: Representation always strains between the real and the ideal.

ANTHONY: Citizens must put the good of the whole ahead of their own. That requires training. To learn the rules of games.

JOSEPHINE: And… how, when necessary, to change those rules.

ANTHONY: They told us we were blue sky dreamers.

JOSEPHINE: It's what it takes to open windows.

ANTHONY: To open doors.

The two of them walk, keep walking, walking, eventually into the din, into the cacophonous chamber of the nation's first sortitionally chosen legislature, the Citizen House.

THE END

A review at either GoodReads or Amazon would be appreciated..

About the author

David Grant has dedicated over four decades to political, cultural and community affairs. Among his accomplishments, in chronological order, are: Master of Fine Arts at the Iowa Writer's Workshop; public television producer-director; self-sufficient homesteader; Peace Corps agro-forester among hunter-gatherers in the Philippines; community organizer with Rural Southern Voice for Peace, developing "The Listening Project"; founder of "Peace Troupe" theater group; educator and trainer in nonviolence for the International Fellowship of Reconciliation; charter director of Nonviolent Peaceforce; founder of Common Lot Productions, exploring improved forms of democracy.

+++++++++

My books about sortition, in different genres and formats, may be found at
http://amazon.com/author/grantd

www.ingramcontent.com/pod-product-compliance
Lightning Source LLC
Chambersburg PA
CBHW020548130626

46552CB00007B/2800